EPHESIAN MIRACLE

EPHESIAN MIRACLE

The Sixth Art West Adventure

Ben and Ann Witherington

PICKWICK *Publications* · Eugene, Oregon

EPHESIAN MIRACLE
The Sixth Art West Adventure

Pickwick Publications
An Imprint of Wipf and Stock Publishers
199 W. 8th Ave., Suite 3
Eugene, OR 97401

www.wipfandstock.com

ISBN 13: 978-1-62032-558-2

Cataloguing-in-Publication data:

Witherington, Ben, 1951–

    Ephesian miracle : the sixth Art West adventure / Ben Witherington III and
Ann Witherington.

    viii + 202 pp. ; 23 cm. Includes bibliographical references.

    ISBN 13: 978-1-62032-558-2

    1. Archaeology—Fiction. I. Witherington, Ann. II. Title.

PS3605 W55 2014

Manufactured in the U.S.A.

For David and Emily Witherington
in celebration of their marriage on October 20, 2012

Contents

1

COINS FOR CHARON

FINGERING THE ANCIENT SILVER coin in his hand, Aziz Mattar realized he was sweating and possibly tarnishing the precious piece of metal, but he didn't care. Just last night he reread in his tattered, leather-bound copy of *Greek Mythology* the story of Charon, the ferryman who steers the souls of the dead across the Styx or Acheron river. The myth always intrigued him.

There had to be a bribe for Charon, otherwise the soul of the dead person wandered for all eternity and never made it into the underworld, a place ruled by Hades, god of the dead. A coin, called the *obol*, was placed on the tongue or the eyes of the deceased so the soul could cross over. And the soul actually wanted to get into the underworld! This was seen as far better than wandering aimlessly along the marshy shore in a limbo-like state, far from the rest of the spirits of the dead.

Standing in the underground cistern across from the site of the ancient Circus Maximus in Istanbul, Aziz could hear the water dripping off the columns in this dark and dank place. An eerie light shone on the column nearby where the jade green head of Medusa could be seen, upside down, at the base of the column. The Byzantines often recycled materials from the earlier Greco-Roman period, in this case to build permanent columns to hold up the ceiling of the cistern.

Soon it would be closing time, and Aziz could get on with his prede-termined ritual and mission. It was not enough to just kill the priest; the discovery of the body must be sensational as well. He had hidden the body of the American-born priest below the water's surface for the moment, weighted down with stones in the darkest corner of the cistern. Few wan-dered this far into the cistern's labyrinth and there were many entryways, including the one hidden in the park behind the cistern which Aziz had used to bring in the body. Now he was just off the approved tourist path, beyond the underground lights that dotted the ceiling and the walkways.

When the bell announced closing for the day, Aziz crouched down behind the Me-dusa head column awaiting the last tour-ist's exit. Though it seemed like forever, it was only five short minutes before the ticket booth closed, and the last guard slammed the creaky metal door at the street side entrance to the cistern before making his rounds.

Aziz sprang into action. Pulling his knife from its sheath he cut the four ropes that bound the aged priest. Quickly, the body floated to the sur-face. Forcing the mouth of the priest open, he placed the silver *obol* on his tongue, and then forced the jaws to shut once more.

With the same sharp curved blade, Aziz made a deep cut in the forehead of the priest, a cut in the shape of a crescent moon. The crescent was perfectly positioned in the center of the priest's forehead which only recently had felt ashes applied to it in the shape of a cross. Opening up a small black book, Aziz chanted as he pushed the corpse out into the watery channel of the cistern.

"Cross over the Acheron to the land of the dead/
may Charon be pleased with the token instead/
go to the place where the infidels dwell/
no journey to heaven, but rather to hell."

Aziz smiled maliciously as the corpse drifted away. Suddenly, Aziz heard the guard's footsteps echoing against the columns. He needed to leave quickly. All the gates would be locked by now, but he had an alternate es-cape route. Taking a deep breath, he lowered himself under the water, swam toward the sluice gate, shimmied through the passageway, and emerged into the larger storm sewer which fed the underwater cistern. As he turned to swim off to the end of the culvert he heard a man screaming from inside the cistern.

A sinister smile came over the face of Aziz. "So begins the retribution of Allah. One down, three to go, double for each of the members of Osama bin Laden's family that died." Then he climbed up the iron steps to the hatch and thence into the park where he would disappear into the lengthening shadows of the evening.

2

WEDDING JITTERS

ART WEST, NEW TESTAMENT scholar and archaeologist, was sitting on the roof balcony of his hotel, the Sea Pines, in Kushadasi watching the cruise ships come and go from the harbor, and the buses load up to head over to the archaeological ruins at Ephesus. The sun was already heating up the air even though it was only seven in the morning on this June day.

 Art was days away from a date with destiny, a destiny named Marissa Okur. He was getting married in the ancient Chora Church in Istanbul by special permission of the Patriarch of Constantinople. They would be spending the first part of their honeymoon in Kushadasi and Art was checking out the hotel to make sure it was up to snuff. Art's response when he was shown the spacious and well-appointed honeymoon suite with a splendid view of the ocean was one word—"Sweet!"

To say Marissa had been busy since Art landed in Turkey a week prior was the understatement of the year. Her family was helping with the wedding arrangements—flowers, dresses, tuxedos, and the dinner and dance cruise on the Bosphorus after the wedding. They were going all out, so thrilled were they that their long single daughter was finally getting married at what they considered the ripe old age of 39. But then her husband to be was no spring chicken either at 52. Balcony sitting provides just the right atmosphere for introspection. His mind swung from "I'm not ready for this" to "It's now or never!"

Art's mother Joyce would be arriving soon from Charlotte along with Jake Arafat and his fiancée, Melody Morris. With basketball season over, Jake and Melody were now planning their own wedding in Wilmington. Art's sister Laura Joyce (or L.J. as the family called her) would be coming from Papua, New Guinea but not before stopping in a variety of exotic cities she always wanted to visit. This would be a four-week holiday, and the beginning of a three-month deserved furlough from her missionary work at the orphanage.

Their friends from Israel would arrive together—Kahlil el Said and his daughter Hannah; Sarah Goldberg, the owner of Solomon's Porch Café; Grace and Manny Cohen and their newly adopted daughter Yelena; and Grayson Johnson, Art's young protégé in Jerusalem.

Dr. James Howell of Myers Park Methodist in Charlotte would conduct the wedding service at the high altar of the Chora Church, surrounded by spectacular mosaics and icons. Several relatives and friends from the States were using the wedding as an excuse to tour the ancient sites of Turkey. They along with everyone else in the wedding were booked into the Anemon Galata Hotel which overlooks the old city center of Istanbul. In some ways Art was just hoping to survive the wedding, never mind enjoy it. He didn't much like crowds or formal occasions like this, but at the same time he knew it was right to celebrate. He prayed it would be an occasion of enormous joy. Art wanted this to please his mother and family, and Marissa and her family as well.

Overhead the sea gulls, hoping for breakfast, were circling the fishing boats heading in from the early morning trawling off the coast of Kushadasi. It was time for Art to come down from the rooftop and have a Mediterranean breakfast. He kept asking himself, is this really going to happen?

With a deep sigh, Art stood up, stretched, and started walking down the steps to the breakfast room several floors below. Who knew that wedding planning could be almost as complicated as conducting an archaeological excavation?

~

Joyce West had always been a stickler for good grooming. Art knew all of her mantras such as "take pride in your appearance" and "clothes make the man." This advice he had practiced with benign neglect from the Beatles era to the present. But Joyce was now to become exhibit A of her own advice, and she dithered about what to wear and how to get her hair done in Charlotte and keep it just right all the way to Istanbul. Mother of the groom might not be as highly rated as mother of the bride, but still this was a big moment in Joyce's life—one of her two children was finally going to get married! She would wear a burka if that was the dress code for weddings in Istanbul!

~

Marissa's palms were sweating, and she wasn't even outdoors. In fact, she was in an air-conditioned room for the last fitting of her wedding gown.

"Now, Miss Okur, stand very still while I put some pins in your dress. Have you lost some weight since I saw you first?" asked Mrs. Hakan, the matronly owner of The Istanbul Bridal Shop on Taksim Square. "That happens to very nervous brides! And your hair? I thought it was much darker—have you changed it? I like this auburn."

"Guilty on both counts," laughed Marissa as she gazed into the mirror. She stood on the platform in a classic creamy lace gown—with a wide peach ribbon around the waist tied up with a bow in the back. "The peach color honors Arthur's southern American roots. He's always talking about peaches—freestone peaches, he calls them—with names like Georgia Belle, Elegant Lady and O'Henry. So I'm going with this peach color. I hope his mother will like it."

"My dear, this gown is a beautiful look for a summer wedding! Elegant enough, but with some slight modifications you can wear this gown to another fancy occasion. That is the smart fashion here today."

Marissa continued to dreamily ponder her image in the mirror as Mrs. Hakan studied every angle and seam. "This is perfect," she sighed. "I think Art will love this dress even though the American style is pure white. Art and his best man are wearing gray tuxedos. It will be beautiful, won't it?" said Marissa seeking validation.

"Child, your taste is impeccable and I know your family will be pleased as well—a mix of the traditional and modern. And your veil is simple too. No heavy Muslim head covering for you! Tell me about your flowers."

"Well that part was easy. Peach roses for everyone with baby's breath mixed in. The girls are wearing paler peach dresses with cream sashes and baby's breath in their hair. Art will have a peach rose of course."

"Of course!" echoed Mrs. Hakan.

Marissa began to fret again. "So much has been done and so many people have to travel so far! Even Art isn't here in Istanbul right now! He's in Kushadasi. So I worry about everything! He must be here soon to meet his mother who is coming all the way from Charlotte in North Carolina."

"Ah, but I know you are a Christian. And I too have learned much about the Christian faith from friends even here in Istanbul. I know you will pray for strength to get through it all, and to deal with whatever happens in the next few weeks. So be of good cheer and rejoice in all things. I pray Allah will be pleased also!"

Marissa laughed. "Yes, I'm sure God is pleased. And God's Apostle Paul said those very words a long time ago to his friends in Thessaloniki who were having more problems than I am!"

"He must have been a very wise man," said Mrs. Hakan with a twinkle in her eye.

3

AN ASIAN ODYSSEY

LAURA JOYCE WAS NOT your ordinary baby sister. In fact, she had a good deal more flair than most missionaries. She had spent the last ten years of her life working in Papua, New Guinea in a Christian orphanage and she welcomed the opportunity to get away for a few months of leave to attend her big brother's wedding. True to form, she decided not to take the easy air route to Istanbul. No, her first stop was Indonesia with its 17,000 islands, one of which is Bali. Luxury trains, buses, and ferries make the scenic trip to Bali's capital of Denpaser very enjoyable. From there she treated herself to the comforts of the Ubud Hanging Gardens Resort. Here she unwound from the years of hard work, enjoying spa treatments, fresh fruit, and the smells of tropical flowers.

With a refreshed body if not also soul, she headed to Kuala Lumpur, the capital of Malaysia. Not really a city girl, she spent only a couple of days in this bustling metropolis of over 1.5 million people. She continued up the peninsula through Bangkok in Thailand and then to Cambodia and

 the city of Siem Reap, the gateway to the Angkor region, to see the beautiful temple referred to as Angkor Wat.

Angkor Wat was built by the Khmer King Suryavarman II in the early 12th century as his state temple and eventual mausoleum. Once Hindu, it is now a Buddhist temple.

From Cambodia Laura flew to Agra, about 125 miles south of Delhi, where she set her sights on the Taj Mahal, the strikingly white marble mausoleum. It was built between  1632 and 1653 by the Mughal emperor Shah Jahan in memory of his third wife, Mumtaz Mahal. Its iconic architecture is known worldwide. Like Angkor Wat, it is a UNESCO World Heritage Site.

Laura decided to stay a few days with missionary friends living nearby, Julie and Timothy Tennent. From there she would slowly make her way to Istanbul.

4

THE LURE OF EPHESOS

EVEN TODAY THERE IS something magical and alluring about the ancient archaeological site of Ephesus, or as the Greeks called it, Ephesos, and as the Turks call it today, Efes. Up to two million now visit the site every year. In the first century, Paul himself walked the streets of Ephesus and John of Patmos immortalized the city as one of the seven churches of his book of Revelation.

Art delivered the rental car to the airport in Izmir after his ninety-minute drive from Kushadasi. On the short flight from Izmir to Istanbul, Art was lost in thought reflecting on the story in the Acts of the Apostles about how Paul upset the silversmiths by referring to their beliefs as religious superstition. A Greek column in Ephesus has a famous inscription wishing the "guild of silversmiths" good fortune. Paul, of course, was busy proclaiming the truth of the Gospel of Jesus Christ. But how does one go about telling the difference between true and false religion, between true and false beliefs and practices involving the supernatural?

Art knew all too well that the difference between miracle and magic had often been debated. Miracle by definition is an act of God, some sort of supernatural or beyond the natural event or occurrence. It should not be seen as something that goes *against* nature, for what sense does it make to say God violated the laws of nature that he set up? But clearly it goes beyond occurrences readily explained by the laws of nature.

Magic, on the other hand, is the human attempt to manipulate not just nature, but also the divine. Whether through astrology or necromancy or spells or curses or potions or rituals or other means, magic in the ancient world was the attempt of humans to use the divine for their various purposes—including healing, influencing the course of events, reversing fates, gaining wealth and much more. The ancients believed there was a spirit world, with spirits both benevolent and malevolent, influencing virtually every aspect of life. The goal of the magi or magician was to determine which spirits were helpful and in what ways. Finally, they would construct a formula or a potion or a spell or a curse which would cause this or that spirit to act on behalf of some particular individual or group.

Through the study of the "demon papyrus," Art and his friend Kahlil[1] learned that there were regular features to ancient magic: 1) complicated rituals; 2) magic spells and recipes; and 3) recitations of the gods' names or even nonsense syllables in hopes of landing on a combination that became words of power, causing the spirit to do one's bidding. In other words, magic involves manipulation and coercion of the spirits—making them an offer they couldn't refuse. Christianity, as portrayed in a text such as Acts 19, the story of Paul in Ephesus, would have appeared as an alternative to popular folk religion of the time, substituting miracles in Jesus' name for magic. Art opened his Greek New Testament and re-read the relevant passage in Acts 19:11–20, translating as he went along.

> God did extraordinary miracles through Paul, so that even handkerchiefs and aprons that had touched him were taken to the sick, and their illnesses were cured and the evil spirits left them.
>
> Some Jews who went around driving out evil spirits tried to invoke the name of the Lord Jesus over those who were demon-possessed. They would say, "In the name of Jesus, whom Paul preaches, I command you to come out." Seven sons of Sceva, a

---

1. A story told in *Papias and the Mysterious Menorah*, the third Art West adventure.

Jewish chief priest, were doing this. (One day) the evil spirit answered them, "Jesus I know, and I know about Paul, but who are you?" Then the man who had the evil spirit jumped on them and overpowered them all. He gave them such a beating that they ran out of the house naked and bleeding.

When this became known to the Jews and Greeks living in Ephesus, they were all seized with fear, and the name of the Lord Jesus was held in high honor. Many of those who believed now came and openly confessed their evil deeds. A number who had practiced sorcery brought their scrolls together and burned them publicly. When they calculated the value of the scrolls, the total came to fifty thousand drachmas. In this way the word of the Lord spread widely and grew in power.

Caption: *St Paul Preaching at Ephesus,* Eustache Le Sueur (1620–1665)

Art's mind wandered for a moment to the famous painting by Eustache Le Sueur of St. Paul preaching in Ephesus showing the magicians burning their magic books. He laughed quietly because, of course, what would have been burned in Paul's day was papyrus scrolls, not leather-bound books!

Jesus could not be manipulated by magicians, and indeed when it was attempted there were negative spiritual consequences for the practitioner! But what about the healing hankies—as Art liked to call them? That certainly sounded like an example of ancient sympathetic magic. Or was it really the case that God's holy presence in Paul could sort of rub off on a piece of cloth and then the cloth be taken to someone in need, so that God's healing power could be conveyed? For Art, this was a puzzling passage in the New Testament. Does God condescend to use our flawed methods of healing out of His love and care for us?

In Art's mind, the difference between miracle and magic was the difference between genuine faith in God and superstition. Superstition believes there are one or more gods that can be manipulated, moved to act by the right set of words or rituals, and the like. In magic, objects and actions are believed to have divine power—a curse tablet, a ritual of sacrifice, etc.

In the case of miracle, the supplicant realizes there is nothing he or she can do to force the divine hand, and so miracle involves asking, but leaving the results in God's hands. And right about now, Art was trying to resist the temptation to try and twist God's arm to produce a certain kind of outcome when it came to his wedding and its celebration. Art did trust the Lord, and after earnest prayer, he now needed to act on that trust, and to stop fretting about the details, including the safety of his sister and mother as they travelled to the wedding.

One thing Art had learned from studying Ephesus in its first century context—real Christianity was rightly seen as a serious threat to the snake oil salesmen, the traders in magic, talismans, sacred replicas and relics in that ancient city. Indeed the stories in Acts 19 emphasize these clashes. Art was hoping for no clashes with members of Marissa's family at their wedding, not least because the ceremony was going to be thoroughly Christian.

Surprisingly, it was Marissa who insisted on including the Eucharist at some point. She wanted them to take their first communion together on the wedding day. However, Muslim guests would see this ceremony as not merely false religion, but as magical in character, and so of the Devil. And to some of Art's low-church Protestant friends it would seem too Orthodox or Catholic for their taste, especially when shared in a setting like the Chora Church.

Art realized they could not please everyone, but he wanted especially to please God and start their marriage off on the right Christian footing. Pretty soon, even with all the human preparation, Art would have to leave the results in God's hands, and that thought gave him some comfort as his plane began the descent into Ataturk Airport.

5

I BELIEVE I CAN FLY

ART'S MOTHER JOYCE, ACCOMPANIED by Jake Arafat her "gentleman lodger" and now famous basketball star for the Charlotte Hornets, along with his fiancée, Melody Morris, had managed to make it safely to JFK in the late afternoon, and the three travelers were sipping Coke Zero in the waiting lounge passing the time until boarding their Turkish Air flight to Istanbul around 7 PM. Joyce was nervous, as it had been a long time since she had done a trans-Atlantic flight, let alone one that lasted 10 hours. She was drinking the Coke to settle her stomach a bit. Melody was chatting away quietly which kept "Aunt Joyce" entertained and her mind off her problems.

Jake could hardly have been more relaxed. He was sprawled out on two chairs listening to Beyoncé on his iPod. Joyce could not understand what the attraction was to singers like Beyoncé, who, in her view, did more screaming than singing. But Beyoncé was also Melody's very favorite non-Christian artist and so when Jake listened to Beyoncé he was also thinking about Melody and Wrightsville Beach. Music has a powerful way of reminding us of important people and places in our lives, as we flash back to where we last heard this or that song. Suddenly the overhead P.A. system interrupted this reverie.

"Ladies and gentleman, the flight to Istanbul is now ready for boarding," announced the Turkish Air attendant at the kiosk next to the breezeway. Joyce bounced up and signaled to Jake it was time to get in line, figuring he couldn't hear a thing with all that music blaring through the ear buds. "Let's get this show on the road," said Joyce mustering up her courage and determination. As Grace would say, she had plenty of chutzpah.

"Okay, okay," said Jake, stretching out his 6'5" frame, yawning, and then standing up. "I've never been to Istanbul you know," he said casually.

"That makes three of us, so we will have ourselves a good adventure, and see if we can't finally get that son of mine married. I was beginning to think you would get married before Art!"

Melody grinned broadly and glanced at the ring on her finger. Suddenly, Jake felt very proud and important, imagining himself a married man like Art. With a flourish he exclaimed, "Ladies, allow me to escort you onto this flight!"

~

Wealth has its advantages, not the least of which is you can travel when you like, especially if you own your own Lear Jet. Such was the case with Grace Cohen, Art's friend and colleague in archaeological work in Israel, and her husband Manny. Both were running around trying to pack so they could head for the Tel Aviv airport by mid-afternoon. Manny's driver brought his company's black limo to the front door of the Cohen compound, all the while drumming his fingers on the steering wheel in tune with his favorite CD, Beyoncé's *I Am—World Tour*. Back in 2009, he traveled to Zagreb to see his favorite singer.

"Did we remember our camera?" asked Grace as she dropped a tube of lipstick into her cosmetic case.

"Yes! What about the wedding gift? Where is it?"

"I've got it in my giant purse which I will personally carry on the plane! Don't forget the navy suit."

"Yes, boss. Remember we can leave when WE are ready—we aren't on a commercial time table! The flight plan is somewhat flexible!"

"Right. Just one more pair of shoes to cram into this bag and I'm done. Remember, we are packing not just for a wedding but a few days of vacation. I've got SO much to show you and Yelena. I will be your personal tour guide. Just wait until you get into that hot air balloon and float over Cappadocia! Hopefully, Yelena will like the Turkish equivalent of an amusement park ride."

To watch this power couple from a distance, you would think they had been doing this routine for years, but in fact they had only been married about three years, and things had gone remarkably well. They had made the necessary adjustments to married life despite their separate careers. They had weathered house renovations and, more importantly, the death of

Grace's Mom. And Yelena had joined their family after being adopted from an orphanage in Siberia.[1] The light of their lives was now snuggled down on a couch listening to music through ear buds.

"So Sarah, Grayson, Kahlil and Hannah are all going to meet us at the airport, right?" asked Manny.

"Absolutely! I'm glad you thought of inviting them to fly with us. That will save them a lot of money. I can't wait to see Grayson all dressed up. I wonder what Yelena will think of him? I doubt they've met." Grayson Johnson, one of the last remaining hippies for Jesus, had been living in Israel and working on various archaeological sites. Thanks to Grace, he was also completing his PhD and would get his diploma next weekend. Seeing Grayson even in a normal suit and tie was as rare as seeing a whale in the Mediterranean these days.

"Come on. Let's scoot," insisted Manny. "I've waited long enough for this wedding and vacation."

"True," quipped Grace, "but some things, like 'moi' for instance, are worth waiting for, would you not agree?"

Manny just smiled as the two ran out the door with now 13-year-old Yelena in the lead yelling, "Is this car big enough for all our stuff?!"

1. A tale told in the Fifth Art West adventure, *Roma Aeterna.*

6

IN THE SHADE
OF THE GALATA TOWER

ISTANBUL IS A JEWEL of a city, the largest in Turkey and fifth largest in the world, with a population over 13 million. Istanbul serves as the cultural and financial center of Turkey, even though the first President, Ataturk, decided that the capital of the country needed to be more centrally located, and hence Ankara was chosen.

Istanbul is unique in that it has neighborhoods both on the European and the Asian sides of the Bosphorus, making it the only metropolis in the world that is situated on two continents. In its long history, Istanbul has served as the capital city of the Roman Empire (330–95), the Eastern Roman or Byzantine Empire (395–1204), the Latin Empire (1204–1261), and the Ottoman Empire (1453–1922). But the city does not rest merely on its ancient laurels. Today it boasts a vibrant cultural and economic world presence.

Most tourists spend their time on the western or European side of the Bosphorus. This area is roughly split into north and south sections by the so-called Golden Horn, a river that opens out into the Bosphorus. Two main bridges connect the north and south areas. Closest to the Bosphorus is the Galata Bridge. Further up river is the Ataturk Bridge.

The Galata Tower traces its ancestry to the Italian people of Genoa who built the tower in 1348 at the highest point of their citadel. You can see it from the air when you fly into the airport, indeed you can see it from most places on the western side of Istanbul. From the Galata Tower, one can walk down the hill, cross the Galata Bridge to the South side of the Golden Horn and soon be in one of the world's largest and oldest covered markets—the Grand Bazaar. Also located on this south side are the Topkapi Palace, the Blue Mosque, and Hagia Sophia. And for museum goers, there's the Istanbul Archaeological Museum with its unparalleled collections spanning almost all of human history.

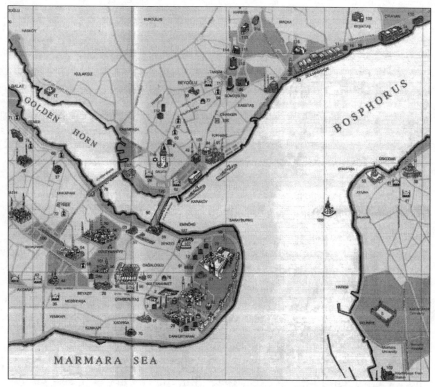

Ekrem Guller was a lifelong resident of Istanbul, indeed a lifelong resident of the neighborhood where the Galata Tower stands. Like many natives of this cosmopolitan city, Guller was an ardent supporter of the arts, and fancied himself one of the better musicians in the city, especially when it came to Turkish jazz. And he looked the part as well. With his jet black wavy hair combed straight back with gel, a goatee and colorful sports shirt, jeans and sandals he appeared to be one laid back dude. Yes, he could also play traditional Turkish music and rock and roll as well, which was still very popular in this town full of clubs and night spots, but lately, besides working in a music store, Ekrem had made most of his living playing at weddings.

Ekrem frequently played piano and vibes and electronic keyboard on the roof garden at the Galata Anemon, which is where Marissa first encountered him. Playing either solo or with a band, Ekrem's life revolved around music. Like so many natives of the larger cities in Turkey, Ekrem was a secular Muslim, a non-observant person of Muslim descent. He was exactly the sort of person Marissa's family felt comfortable with orchestrating the music for the dinner cruise, and that was important, because they were apprehensive as to how some of the family would react to Marissa not only marrying a Christian, but having a Christian wedding service in a national monument like the Chora Church.

In a smart move, Marissa's family had decided that their observant Muslim relatives and friends would be invited only to the cruise, not to the wedding service itself. On this morning, Marissa and Ekrem were drinking cups of Turkish coffee and discussing the music for the cruise.

"So you are saying that you will provide two hours of music, a tasteful mixture of traditional Turkish music, show tunes that the older folks can dance to, a little rock n' roll, and some jazz towards the end of the cruise?"

"Yes, of course, Miss Okur. A little something for everyone and every taste in music!" promised Ekrem.

"Excellent! Now you realize it will take us until about 6 P.M. just to get everyone on the boat after the wedding at 4? Of course, perhaps fifty or so will be coming directly to the boat between 5 and 6 since they are not coming to the wedding service. Will you be able to entertain them while they have drinks and wait for the wedding party?"

"Yes, we can do that as well for an extra 500 lira."

"That's totally fine. I understand." Mentally doing the math, Marissa figured this amounted to about $800 (1500 lira) total plus tip, which was about what she and Art had budgeted for this part of the wedding festivities. She rationalized that she would be only doing this once, so better to do it well.

"What do we do if it rains? Are you prepared to move everything inside the boat, and how long would that take?"

"Trust me," said Ekrem. "We have coped with every imaginable kind of condition at wedding receptions and parties. Once we were playing for a reception right on the shore of the Bosphorus in a park, and all of a sudden there was a huge thunder storm and a flash flood, and we moved everything in about twenty minutes to a nearby covered market on higher ground and just kept playing."

"Yes I heard about that flash flood—twenty people lost their lives that day in 2009, did they not?"

"Indeed. It was a sad day," said Ekrem shaking his head. "So moving from one part of the boat to another is no big deal at all—it would take fifteen minutes at most."

Marissa began to relax a little bit. "Don't forget that Art and I have chosen the Journey song "Faithfully" for our first dance, so I hope you have a decent vocalist for that. It's a challenging song requiring a high tenor."

"In fact we have a nice soprano who will sing that for you—Acelya Demir. Perhaps you have heard of her? She is very popular here in Istanbul."

"The name rings a bell, but no I don't think I've heard her. Saying goodbye to Ekrem, Marissa headed down to the lobby. She strolled through the front door, crossed the narrow, cobblestoned street, and sat in the small park in front of the hotel, beside the tower.

"I just hope the weather stays this nice," murmured Marissa to herself as she gazed up at the 9-story medieval stone tower. "We have got to find the time to take our guests up to the tower restaurant. I know they'll love the view of the Bosphorus from up there. And maybe the younger crowd can enjoy the nightclub too."

She tried to imagine what the original builders would think of today's use of the Tower. After all, it was erected in 1348 when Istanbul was still called Constantinople. And it was named the Tower of Christ! At 220 feet, it was their version of a sky scraper! She doubted that Muslims in Turkey today were aware of its Christian history. But then Turkey is filled with Christian history—maybe someday Christianity will rise again, she thought. For now she would settle for more openness between the faiths.

7

THE GALATA GANG

THE ROOM WAS SMALL, cramped, and smelled of mold and cigarette smoke. The five folding chairs arranged into a circle were near the grimy window of this tenth floor flat so there would be enough light to see. Officially, no one lived in this apartment and had not for some time, which made it a perfect rendezvous place for Aziz and his friends. No one could trace them to this location which overlooked the Galata Tower.

Aziz was insufferably pleased with himself. He could not brag enough to his four partners about what he accomplished the previous day. What was especially surprising about Aziz was not merely his relish for violence, but also his ardor for radical Islamic ideas, despite being well educated in the many cultures and religions of Turkey, both modern and ancient. He was prepared to use his knowledge of ancient cultures and mythology in the service of Islam, which to an outsider would have seemed an odd combination. But Aziz was smart enough to send mixed messages to his opponents. When they examined the corpse of the priest they would find not only a crescent wound on his head, but an ancient *obol* in his mouth.

The headlines in the various Istanbul papers, both in Turkish and English, regaled one and all with the grisly nature of the murder of an elderly Catholic priest, Father Donovan. Even Turkey's President, Abdullah Gül, weighed in and said this would require an urgent and thorough investigation. But they would discover that the trail had gone cold, and the water in the cistern would have removed all evidence of fingerprints. In Aziz's mind a perfect crime had been committed, and this emboldened him to think he could continue his "deeds of righteousness against the infidels" as he called them.

Aziz was noted for his considerable moustache. Born and raised in the far eastern end of Turkey in the town of Van (on Lake Van) near the border with Iran, Aziz had been a militant Muslim since he was young. He had only disgust for the so-called secular Muslim ethos of much of Turkey, especially its urban centers like Istanbul. His ire was especially keen against Christians, two of whom he helped martyr two years prior. Now he had been brought into the Circle of Five, a small coven of radical Islamists in Istanbul, to help them accomplish their aims, namely stirring up anger against the Westernizing and Christianizing of Turkey.

Aziz's four fellow zealots, Ekrem, Gabir, Huseyin, and Iskender, while they had some courage, nevertheless had never killed anyone, so Aziz was brought in as the hit man. Iskender, whose name means defender of men, was the intellectual leader of the group, and he smiled as he spoke to Aziz.

"You have done well my brother, but we have bigger plans as you know. You have shown you are capable of great acts of courage. Our targets are not just Western Christians. We must strike terror into the secular heart of our land, and so we plan to target secular Muslims as well."

"It does not matter to me. Secular Turks are the worst betrayers of Islam, and they deserve their fate. It is important that we carry on with these deeds of righteousness against infidels if we are to accomplish our main goal. We must prevent Turkey from becoming part of the European Union, and so becoming even further allied with the West instead of with our fellow Muslims in the Middle East! I grow weary of seeing all the Western tourists walking around this neighborhood staying in the hotels. Our nation has become too dependent on tourism, especially from America and Europe. Too many Germans, too many Americans! It cannot come to any good end, and all just for money—money!"

"Our country has no principles any more. It spurns Sharia law. Even our women do not have to wear burkas or be veiled—it is a scandal!" chimed in Ekrem.

Aziz had a personal stake in all these things, which had shaped his views. His own sister repudiated radical Islam, entered the university here in Istanbul, and had become a liberated woman, even something of a feminist. Aziz could hardly bear to mention her Arabic name—Fatma—which ironically means abstinence. He spat it out, because in Aziz's mind she was a prostitute, dating Westernized Turks and even Westerners here in Istanbul. "So let's talk about our hit list," said Aziz with relish.

"Ah yes, the Orthodox priest, Father Demetrios. It's a nice touch that he works so closely with the Patriarch himself. After these two executions, it will be clear we are targeting Christians."

"And speaking of Christians, I noticed something interesting in this morning's paper," inserted Huseyin. "I thought that the Chora Church had long since ceased to be used as a church and now was just a national museum, rather like Hagia Sophia."

"You are right to think this way," said Iskender. "Why?'

"Because someone has given permission to hold a Christian wedding in this church—a wedding between Professor Marissa Okur from Ankara and some teacher from America, a man named Arthur West."

"And when will this wedding take place?" asked Iskender.

"This Saturday!" replied Huseyin.

"Something must be done about this—something that will send a signal far and wide," asserted Aziz.

"What do you have in mind?" asked Ekrem a bit cautiously.

"I don't know yet, but I'll think of something. I always do," stressed Aziz with a smile that revealed a broken front tooth. "Just last year . . . "

Iskender interrupted, "We'll worry about that later. Right now, I need to know if you are ready for tomorrow."

"Yes, yes! I will meet Father Demetrios for coffee in the morning. The fool thinks I'm ready to convert!" The Circle of Five laughed uproariously at the irony until Aziz finally continued.

"We will have a nice chat by the Bosphorus—the last one he will ever have, if all goes well."

"*Ensh'allah* [As Allah wills]," replied Iskender still smiling.

8

THE HOUSE OF THE VIRGIN MARY

THE PATRIARCH, A SPIRITUAL leader of the world's Eastern Orthodox Christians, was at his wits end. He held in his hand the scientific confirmation that caused both excitement and dread to arise in his heart—a forensic DNA report on the remains of a body that was tested recently in great secrecy. The report made clear that the bones were those of a woman from the first century A.D., and the remaining hair sample made clear she was from the Near East, closer to Israel, not Turkey. The remains were found in a crypt beneath a house known as the House of the Virgin Mary. According to one tradition, the mother of Jesus resided here after being brought to Turkey by the Beloved Disciple. Also, according to one tradition she ascended into heaven, *bodily*, from this very spot!

 Who was the woman found buried beneath this little shrine that stood upon the ruins of an ancient house? The Patriarch knew that even if it was the body of Jesus' mother, some Christians would not flinch at this news, Protestants in particular. But for Catholics and the Orthodox, like the Patriarch, this was a huge problem.

According to the belief of Christians of the Roman Catholic Church, Eastern Orthodoxy, Oriental Orthodoxy, and parts of the Anglican

Communion, the Assumption of Mary was the bodily ascension of the Virgin Mary into heaven at the end of her life. The Roman Catholic Church teaches as dogma that the Virgin Mary "having completed the course of her earthly life, was assumed body and soul into heavenly glory." This doctrine was infallibly defined by Pope Pius XII on November 1, 1950, in his Apostolic Constitution *Munificentissimus Deus*. The Pope chose not to commit the church to saying that the Assumption occurred before or after her actual death, but the majority opinion is that the Assumption occurred immediately after death.

The Eastern Orthodox churches support a slightly different option known as the Dormition of the Theotokos. In this view, Mary died and her soul was taken to heaven. Three days later, her body was assumed into heaven also as a preview of the coming resurrection of all Christians. In the churches that believe either viewpoint, the Assumption is a major feast day, commonly celebrated on August 15. For the Orthodox, such as Patriarch Bartholomew I, this was a big religious festival.

"Suppose," said the Patriarch to himself, sipping his coffee and twisting his garnet colored episcopal ring as he sat in his study, "it is true, that these are the actual bones of Mary? Then what? Do I ask for a full and open inquiry into the matter, in which case it will become public? Do I bury this information, and hide behind the façade that after all we cannot be sure it really is Mary?" The Patriarch began stroking and pulling at his beard, oblivious to his surroundings.

Now Bartholomew was an honest man. He knew that nothing could be theologically true that was historically false especially when it comes to an historical religion like Christianity. Indeed, he himself was passionate about history, hence his moral dilemma.

But it was not just that an ancient woman's corpse had been found beneath the shrine. It was what was buried with her that troubled him even more. Had there just been a corpse, and nothing more, he might have been able to reconcile it with his conscience to simply file away this information and think no more about it. The problem was more complex because a rather large golden pendant was found around the neck of the corpse. And when the pendant was carefully pried open there was a very tiny piece of rolled up papyrus inside. And on the papyrus were the following words in Aramaic:

Maryām buried here
By the disciple whom Jesus loved

Suppose it was *not* true that Mary had followed the example of her son Jesus with a bodily ascension into heaven? In some ways this would be more problematic for the Catholics than for the Orthodox because the Pope had made it a Catholic dogma, a non-negotiable belief. The Orthodox accepted this tradition, but since most Orthodox Churches had no Pope (the Coptic Church being an exception) there had never been such a pronouncement by a singular head of the Orthodox Church. But Orthodox believers are just as passionate about their post-biblical traditions as the Catholics, and take them as dogma just as much as the Catholics do.

Taking another sip of coffee, the Patriarch flipped through pictures of the pendant. When the pendant was cleaned, something else came to light—it was engraved with an image of Mary herself clinging to the cross! Perhaps the Beloved Disciple commissioned this piece from one of the skilled artisans who worked in gold and silver in Ephesus. Or perhaps it had been added after the fact, by some custodian of the grave.

There was much to do—a study of some sort had to be conducted by thoroughly trustworthy experts. For now, the Patriarch decided to do nothing about this potential bombshell. Very few people knew about the find. Of course, there were the archaeologists who made the discovery but were, for now, leaving the announcements in the hands of their highly-respected Patriarch. There was also his closest confidant, Father Demetrios, whom he could trust with his very life.

He would think about whether there was anyone else he trusted, Turkish or not. It must be someone who was an ecumenical Christian like himself; someone who knew history and theology; someone with archaeological experience. But who? Perhaps it would come to him after more prayer.

9

ALL ABOARD!

KAHLIL EL SAID COULD still hardly believe he was literally riding with the jet set heading to a wedding in Istanbul. Growing up in Jerusalem, he remembered vividly the creaky oxcart he rode in as a child, sharing the space with the harvested crops heading to the market in Jerusalem. As a child his mental horizons had never gone beyond life in Palestine. His father never left the country, and indeed never flew in an airplane, and yet here was Kahlil doing both on the same day. Truly he saw himself as a blessed man in his golden years—a successful owner of a well-known antiquities shop, and now a grandfather. Hannah, his daughter, doted on son Samuel who was safe with the babysitter for this trip. He knew, however, that Hannah was fretting because this was the first time mother and son had been apart. He promised himself to be attentive to his daughter.

People had often said he looked like Omar Sharif with his handsome face and thick wavy hair and moustache, now all silver, and his deep booming voice and big smile. But he doubted that even Omar, also a Muslim, would have such a plane. "What is most amazing to me about this plane is how very quiet it is, unlike so many planes, especially the ones that still have propellers."

"Indeed," said Manny Cohen, "it's one of the big selling features of this plane. Sorta like the whisper jet because you can hear a whisper in this plane. I'd say it comes down to having very good insulation! This Lear is one of the larger versions with 12 seats. I have to admit we use it a lot in my computer business."

Grayson Johnson, who was sitting near Kahlil and Hannah, was in awe of the silver bird. "For sure, this is way better than flying El Al. I'm convinced the seats are getting smaller on those big jets!" laughed Grayson whose lanky frame was filling out a bit. "I wish the trip was longer—two hours just isn't gonna cut it. We're even in the same time zone with Istanbul! I could fly all day in this baby!"

Grayson had been Art West's assistant on several digs in the Holy Land, and now was in charge of a quadrant of the dig at Caesarea Philippi. On top of that he was about to get his Ph.D. Still sporting his trademark shoulder length hair and ever-present jeans, today he also wore a rainbow-colored, short-sleeve shirt which revealed a tattoo on his right forearm which read *en arche ho logos*—In the beginning was the Word. Yelena, who had never met a bona-fide hippie, was in awe! But Grayson was used to stares. Even Sarah was giving him longer-than-usual glances. He was too embarrassed to return the favor; Sarah was someone he always admired from afar. Coffee at Solomon's Porch, especially if personally served by Sarah, was not to be missed when he was on Ben Yehuda Street. Grayson smiled as he thought about Sarah's smile, and looked over just in time to catch her glance up again. Sighing, he moved to an empty seat closer to Grace.

"Professor Levine, can you tell me what you think about the idea of the Emperor cult setting up shop right here at the edge of the Holy Land in Caesarea Philippi?" asked Grayson.

"Well, I am not entirely shocked by this, especially after seeing that pagan altar which was recently uncovered at Beit She'an. I think it confirms a pagan presence especially on the perimeter of the Holy Land. Of course, Caesarea Philippi had once been the Greek town called Banyas/Panyas, named after the Greek god Pan, so we should not be surprised at finding an Emperor cult in such places."

Grayson sighed, "But why did Jesus take a little field trip with his inner circle to Caesarea Philippi? And he even revealed his identity to his disciples there! Seems kinda deliberate to me. Man, is he suggesting he is the messianic figure, the savior figure? Is he saying the Emperor and these other Greek gods are so NOT such figures?"

"Well, it's an interesting theory, and it might explain why on occasion Jesus hushed his followers and even the supposed demons when they began to reveal who he was. It might be seen as treason in some minds."

Just then a pleasant female voice came over the intercom with a list of gourmet snacks to tide them over on the two-hour flight. The flight attendant then appeared with trays of hors d'oeuvres, fruits and cheeses, and petit fours.

"I've died and gone to heaven," laughed Kahlil to Hannah.

10

WHAT'S IN THE COFFEE?

THE LIGHT BREEZE BLOWING across the Bosphorus made sitting by the bay quite pleasant at this hour of the morning. Father Demetrios was an elderly priest whose flock involved a large sector of Istanbul. He was one of the most revered figures in the city, a gentle and quiet man who always had a kind word for everyone, Christian or not. He was also Patriarch Bartholomew's confessor and confidant; and the only other person outside the archaeologists themselves who knew about the discovery at the shrine of Mary.

When Aziz called the priest, he quite readily agreed to the meeting, for Aziz had used a family name on Father Demetrios' own church roles. Aziz told the good priest that he had finally decided to convert to the Orthodox faith and wanted counsel and baptism into the church. This was such a rare and exciting request that Father Demetrios had been all too happy to meet with Aziz. Iskender's spies had done their research and he knew the priest was basically addicted to coffee, in particular, hazelnut cream coffee.

Aziz would meet the priest at the café, buy the coffee, lace it with cyanide, and then guide the priest to a pleasant park bench alongside the Bosphorus. The strong coffee should easily hide the almond taste. Symptoms would strike rapidly—shortness of breath and then cardiac arrest. All this Aziz knew, which meant he needed to get the priest to the park bench before he drank his coffee.

Fingering his ring, a very interesting ring with a crescent diamond chip in the center which sparkled in the sun, Aziz was nervous. What if the priest did not come? What if someone saw him dose the coffee? These thoughts raced through his mind even as he looked up and saw an elderly man in a black robe and hat walking with a cane toward the Bosphorus Café.

Walking toward him, Aziz said in a friendly voice, "You must be Father Demetrios. How kind of you to come on such short notice."

"Not at all," replied the feeble voice, "I am always happy to do the Lord's work, my son."

"Of course, of course! I will go get us some coffee, and then we can sit on one of those benches in the park. I would like our conversation to be most private. Which kind would you like today?"

"I am rather partial to their hazelnut blend here, caffeinated of course. I don't understand people who drink coffee without the caffeine. What is the point, I ask myself? That's like drinking non-alcoholic wine. It makes no sense to me!" shared the cleric with a laugh.

"I totally agree," replied Aziz affably. "I'll be right back, and we can talk." After about four minutes of waiting in line, and then waiting for the coffee, Aziz extracted the potent vial from his inside coat pocket, and poured the liquid into the priest's coffee, stirring both drinks carefully before leaving the café."

"Let me carry the coffee to our bench," offered Aziz. "We can talk on the way."

"Yes, let me hear your story my boy! How is it you came to seek baptism into our church? You know of course that Istanbul was once Constantinople, the very heart and capital of the Christian world, and we like to think it still is."

"Well, Father, it is a rather strange story. I have always been a spiritual and zealous person, but only recently has my focus turned more towards Christianity. I grew up next to Lake Van in the far eastern portion of our country."

"Ah yes, it was terrible when those Christians out there were martyred a couple of years ago. Just terrible! I attended the memorial funeral in Izmir, and it was a sad occasion to say the least."

"Do you believe that martyrs go directly to heaven?" inquired Aziz.

"Yes, I do."

"Tell me, Father. What are the essential things one must believe to be a Christian?"

"One must believe in Jesus Christ as truly man and truly God and believe in his crucifixion and resurrection as the means of the world's salvation."

"Yes, and what else," asked Aziz pointedly.

"Believe in the Holy Trinity; the Bible as the Word of God for His people; the great Creeds of the Church; the Orthodox traditions. These are weighty subjects for the convert to ponder over time," cautioned the priest.

"Yes, yes, but what must I do to be saved?" asked Aziz, who was becoming increasingly agitated as they neared the park bench.

"You must repent of your sins, my son and believe that Jesus is your savior."

"Ah, here is the bench I had in mind," said Aziz trying to calm himself.

Once seated, the priest sighed and said, "The breeze is delicious at this time of day in the park. It is so pleasant to see the boats on the Bosphorus."

"And the coffee will be delicious also," said Aziz as he handed the priest the lethal cup. By now Father Demetrios was eager for his morning coffee and drank it readily.

Then Aziz stared straight into the priest's face. "Are you ready to be a martyr for your faith?" he asked rather coldly, fingering his crescent ring.

The priest looked at him strangely and then . . . his breath became shorter as he swayed with dizziness. Seconds later he seized up and fell forward. Aziz caught him as he went into cardiac arrest. He propped the body back against the bench, and sat beside him quietly. From a distance it would look as if the old man was just sleeping in the sunshine.

Taking out his cigarette lighter, he heated up the crescent diamond on his ring and then strongly pressed the symbol into the center of the old man's forehead, holding it there for about a full minute. The noxious smell of burning flesh wafted its way into his nose, and a small close-lipped smile came upon Aziz's face. He could easily see the little crescent moon mark, a rising red welt on the forehead of the priest. Then he slipped the *obol* coin into his mouth.

"That's two down, and plenty to go," said Aziz as he sauntered away quickly and headed towards the shops under the Galata Bridge where he disappeared into the crowd.

11

HOTELS AND MORE

LAURA JOYCE WAS BONE weary when she finally got out of the taxi in Istanbul. Sure enough, the famous Pera Palace Hotel was just as advertised—an ornate Victorian abode with lots of brass and chandeliers and high ceilings. L.J. rode the glass-walled elevator up to the Agatha Christie room, feeling as though she was in a movie. She was the only person in the immediate wedding party not staying at the Galata Anemon, as she wanted to live out her fantasy of following in the footsteps of Hercule Poirot. Little did she realize when she set out on her journey that fictional characters have far more stamina than real middle-aged persons, but she was feeling that reality now!

The bellhop with the little red flat tam on his head had snatched up her suitcase and was accompanying her on her journey to her room. When they reached the second floor landing, he informed her, "Miss Agatha's room is right here; President Ataturk stayed at the end of the hall."

Laura Joyce had paid a pretty penny to stay in this hotel for two nights, but she was ever so glad that it was quiet now that the door was shut, and that the huge four-poster bed surprised her with a mattress that was soft as a baby's bottom. Almost instantly she fell asleep, unworried about clocks and time schedules. Little did she know that there was planned for 9 p.m. a murder mystery dinner downstairs in the dining room, complete with phony gunshots and screams. But for the moment, she was sleeping the sleep of the dead, and dreaming about the Taj Mahal. Istanbul seemed positively cool compared to that stop in India.

~

The melodic ring tones of a Bach cantata suddenly alerted Marissa to an incoming call.

"This is Art checking in with wedding central," said the voice on the other end of the line. "I can report the safe arrival of three guests—Mom, Jake and Melody!"

"Good going, Art," laughed Marissa! "I'm glad to hear your family has begun to arrive. I will meet you here in the hotel lobby. Any word from your sister?"

"She's a missionary woman on a different mission—to stay at the Pera Palace Hotel. So I'm expecting a call from her soon, I hope! But with Laura, anything can happen!"

All our friends from Jerusalem checked in last night but I think they are out sightseeing right now. Hopefully, we can all get together for dinner here. Regardless, keep me posted!" said Marissa as she checked off another item on her to-do list.

"Roger, over and out," replied Art.

~

The staff at the Galata Anemon Hotel had become used to seeing the men come into the hotel, ride the elevator up to the roof garden, and sit around a table for five. Some of these men they recognized from the neighborhood but one in particular they had not seen before, and with good reason. Gabir was fresh out of Soganlik, the most infamous of all prisons in the vicinity of Istanbul.

The waiters in the lounge gave them a wide berth. Thus far, no trouble had come from their presence, but there was gossip among the staff that the manager had been paid off by these five so they could come and go as they pleased. Yes, they paid for their drinks and snacks, but they seldom left tips. They just demanded service—over and over again. And service they got, but without any smiles.

12

BISHOPS DOWN

Aziz sat quietly staring at his chessboard, a cigarette stub hanging from his large lips. No one besides himself in the Circle of Five played chess, and he did so to relieve stress while sitting in the park near his flat. For some reason killing two Christian priests had not calmed him down. To the contrary, it had revved him up for more. On his chessboard the two white bishops had been captured and eliminated, and in his mind they represented the twin killings of the Christian priests. As he stared at the chessboard he realized the ultimate goal would be capturing the queen and king. And he knew just the queen and king he wanted to target.

~

President Abdullah Gül was not a happy camper. At present he was sitting in his palatial office high above Ankara yelling through the telephone at Istanbul's police chief Kagan Koksal. Yet another priest had been found dead, this time by a fisherman in the park along the Bosphorus. The immediate cause of death was heart-attack but the reason for the heart attack wouldn't be official until the autopsy results were in. Still—two priests in two days. He didn't believe in coincidence any more than his police chief did. They were convinced both men were murdered by the same killer. The timing of this was atrocious as Istanbul was about to host a major European soccer tourney, plus an International Jazz Festival. The Turkish economy needed tourism from the West to increase not decrease, and these grisly murders of priests could really put a damper on things.

Already the story of the first murder victim, found floating in the cistern near the very heart of the tourist district, had become front page news not only in the English language Turkish paper, but also in the Herald-Tribune. And the Reuters reporter made sure that the story circulated back to the U.S. and all over Europe. Now there was a second similar killing, with the similar death mark—the crescent on the forehead—making it look like an Islam-conquers-Christianity statement.

Little evidence has been found at either site to suggest a suspect. Even a lengthy interrogation of the local who found the second priest had produced no composite sketch of a possible killer. An olive-skinned man with black hair and a mustache was not a suspect description worth even a hundred lira in a city full of such men. Hopefully, soon, someone or some group would claim responsibility to reap the publicity.

"I'm telling you we have got to track this killer down before the beginning of the soccer tournament. These murders are giving the city a black eye, which up to now had a reputation of being a safe and inviting place for citizens and tourists alike. Furthermore, it may slow our efforts to become part of the European Union. Fix this!"

"Yes, Mr. President, I hear you loud and clear," said a weary Chief Koksal. "We have our best detectives on the case, so please be patient."

"My patience is running out, and there's no end of potential victims in your neighborhood. Put a stop to this criminal, by whatever means necessary. I want these headlines to disappear!"

"Yes, Mr. President, I will keep in touch," promised the Chief.

As the phone went dead, the President's secretary approached saying, "You need to see this story sent over by one of our contacts with the tabloids. It will be run tomorrow." The headline read, "Gül Too Gullible about the Safety of Istanbul?" A picture of the President frantically running his hand through his hair accompanied the article. And as he stared at his picture, the secretary beat a hasty retreat out of his office.

13

THE CHORA CHURCH

IT WOULD BE HARD to over-estimate the beauty of the Chora Church. Situated today on a narrow street in a densely populated neighborhood in the historic part of Istanbul, this church is today a tourist attraction called the Kariye Museum. But it was not always so. Marissa was proofreading the final copy of a pamphlet they would give their guests. The pamphlet, complete with pictures, read . . .

The Chora Church was originally built in the early fifth century outside the walls of Constantinople, south of the Golden Horn. The church's full name in Greek was the Church of the Holy Savior in the Country. However, when Theodosius II built his formidable walls in 413–14, the church became incorporated within the city's defenses, but kept the name *Chora* which means country.

The current building dates from 1077–1081 but over the years there has been much in the way of refurbishing and redecorating. Most of the mosaics date to the Byzantine period in the 1300s. The artists remain unknown.

Around fifty years after the fall of the city to the Ottomans, the Chora Church was converted into a mosque—*Kariye Camii*. The mosaics and frescoes were covered with a layer of plaster. This and frequent earthquakes have taken their toll.

In 1948, Thomas Whittemore and Paul A. Underwood, from the Byzantine Institute of America and the Dumbarton Oaks Center for Byzantine Studies, sponsored a program of restoration. From that time on, the building ceased to be a functioning mosque. In 1958, it was opened to the public as a museum—*Kariye Müzesi*.

So it was that Marissa had suggested this as the site for the wedding. Art managed to get a special dispensation to have a wedding there. They both loved the beautiful iconic mosaics, the vaulted ceiling, and the excellent acoustics in the central nave. What a perfect and memorable place to have their wedding ceremony. Dr. James Howell from Charlotte might find it hard to concentrate on the wedding ceremony he was conducting!

The press planned to cover it in some detail. This would provide endless fodder for the local gossip columns. What sort of important people could persuade the Patriarch and the President of Turkey to allow a wedding in a national museum?

Though officially a secular country, Turkey nonetheless had laws that discouraged Christians from worshipping outright. For example, the Orthodox school for training priests housed on a small island next to Istanbul had been closed for decades, thus preventing the training of such priests anywhere in Turkey. While the government claimed that this was because all private schools of any kind were closed almost fifty years ago, the truth was that this policy was specifically set up so that the religious life in Turkey could be governmentally controlled in various ways. The government did not want any sort of fundamentalists, as they called them, gaining a foothold in Turkey.

This made the special dispensation for Art's wedding all the more surprising. What the press did not know is that the Ministry of Tourism had stepped in to make this possible not merely because of Marissa's connections and involvement with them, but because that Ministry wanted more Christian tourists to visit Turkey, and wanted Turkey to continue to 'appear' to be a free and open society. And behind the Ministry of Tourism's intervention was in fact a phone call from the President, seeing this as a positive P.R. opportunity, urging the Ministry to do what it could to help facilitate this wedding in the Chora Church.

Both Art and Marissa had refused interviews with the various papers, doing their best to keep a low profile, but still the latest wedding details were appearing in the papers on a daily basis. Thus, Aziz was able to keep track of what was happening, and now he knew exactly when and where the wedding of these famous, or in his mind infamous, infidels would take place.

~

Sitting in the roof garden at the Galata Anemon waiting for his circle of friends to show up, Aziz was suddenly startled by a young man who rushed out of the elevator obviously looking for someone. Seeing only Aziz, he asked in Turkish, "You wouldn't know where Dr. Marissa Okur might be would you? I've got to nail down some last minute details for the Bosphorus cruise."

Smiling, Aziz said smoothly, "I'm afraid I can't help you with that, but you say Dr. Okur and Professor West will be cruising?"

The young musician, Ekrem Guller, beamed proudly. "Yes! After the wedding! And I personally am providing the music. It will be a wonderful cruise on the Bosphorus!"

"Well, I am sure it will be! Do you have a business card? I may be in need of your services," replied Aziz continuing to ingratiate himself with the musician.

"Of course, sir!" And having handed over his business card, he scurried off.

And now Aziz's thoughts turned in a whole different direction. There would be no need to interfere with the wedding or cause a scene at the hotel. But when everyone's guard was down and there was too much alcohol flowing on a cruise boat, all kinds of things were possible. "Perfect," murmured Aziz, "just perfect."

14

UNEXPECTED GUESTS

SHE SENT IN THEIR RSVP card to Marissa Okur, but forgot to sign it. Christy and David Herring were Art West's twin first cousins once removed, children of his first cousin, Kathy. Both in their mid-twenties and fresh out of graduate school each with a Master's Degree from Duke, they were taking a well-deserved vacation before job hunting. Christy was all about books; David was all about computers; both enjoyed travel.

For the past month they backpacked their way through Europe all the while planning to be in Istanbul for the wedding. Just now they were in a hotel in Thessaloniki, trying to book passage across the Aegean and through the Dardanelles to Istanbul. Apparently, there were not many passenger boats going their way, and trains no longer run between Greece and Turkey. Christy was getting increasingly frustrated with the lack of help from the concierge at the hotel desk. "So what you are saying is, take a twelve-hour minimum bus trip and there's only one bus a day and it's already left!"

"Unless you want to fly," said the tall thin man with little patience for young Americans. Sweeping her dark hair back from her brow, Christy thought about this for a moment. She and her brother didn't have the funds for a flight.

Just then a middle-aged, blonde-haired gentleman came up to the desk. He was obviously some kind of tour group leader complete with an official jacket and clipboard. Speaking to the same clerk he said, "We'll be leaving for Turkey within the hour and we need to settle up with you about the incidental charges. Do we have any to speak of?"

When he finished and turned to leave, Christy said, "I couldn't help but overhear that your group is on the way to Turkey. Are you heading straight to Istanbul first?"

"Why yes," said the blonde haired man with a smile. "Why do you ask?"

Summoning up a lot of courage she blurted, "Do you have a couple of spare seats for two Americans who desperately need to get to Istanbul for a wedding? We could pay a little something!"

Laughing, the man answered, "Actually—we do! But we haven't been properly introduced. My name is Rick Sanders, tour host for Ellene Tours. And you are . . . ?"

"Christy Ann Herring. My twin brother David and I have been backpacking through Europe and now we are going to my cousin's big wedding at the Chora Church in Istanbul!" said Christy with a huge smile on her face.

"Not the now-famous wedding of Professor Art West!? I just read about it in the Herald-Tribune. It will be the first wedding in Chora Church in ages. We had to rearrange our schedule to visit the museum because of his wedding. It's amazing that I would just accidentally run into some of West's wedding guests here in Thessaloniki. I watch his TV show on archaeology, and this tour group is basically Christians on pilgrimage through the Lands of the Bible."

"Oh I doubt it's a matter of pure chance," replied Christy with a grin, "more like the providence of God."

"Right you are, right you are! Well, have your things ready in an hour and we will be leaving this seaport town and heading north by northeast. I guarantee my bus driver knows the way!"

Christy quickly ran up the stairs to find David who was busy blogging and twittering. "Dave! I've got a techie job for you! Contact Cousin Art and tell him we are on the way! I found us a ride!"

15

HOME, SWEET HOME

THE AUSTRIANS ARE NOTHING if not thorough and meticulous. And such is the case when it comes to the archaeological work at Ephesus that has been going on for over a century. While casual tourists might focus on the library of Celsus or the theater where the protest against St. Paul once took place, the most spectacular archaeological work being done in Ephesus in recent years has to do with the slope or terrace houses. Ever careful, the Austrians built an elaborate roof structure over these terraced houses to protect them from the sunlight and other elements. Now it requires a separate ticket to get into this special exhibition in "downtown" Ephesus, but it is well worth it.

 Set in tiers on a hill that overlooks Ephesus' main street, this was the high rent district in the age of Paul and later. Art had been one of the first to see and photograph these houses which revealed what had already been assumed, namely that Ephesus was a town with lots of very wealthy people.

Art was busy distracting himself from the impending event in his life. The best way Art knew to quell his fears was to focus on something else he loved—namely archaeological work at Ephesus. He started scrolling through his latest pictures of the terrace houses taken a few days before, all the while typing up his notes for an article to be published soon.

"Particularly interesting are the frescoed images of philosophers on the walls of house number 2. The wealthy were also the most literate in the area. This find rivals the ones at Pompeii and Herculaneum in uncovering daily life of the well-to-do."

Clicking on the next picture, he typed, "Note the mosaic of Dionysius and Ariadne, two popular figures from Greek mythology and religion, Dionysius being the God of wine and celebration."

Art was now considering multiple articles, one on each house, based on the incredible number of great pictures he had taken. "It would be a

good excuse to go back and take more pictures! I wonder if Marissa would be up for that—on the honeymoon," mused Art as he started typing again.

"By far, the most interesting room in this house has been called the theater room, based on the theatrical subjects of its frescoes. One of the owners of the house may well have overseen theater performances in Ephesus for a living. The right-hand wall has a scene from Menander's comedy, *Perikeiromene* ("The Girl Who Gets her Hair Cut"), and the left

wall bears a scene from Euripides' *Orestes*. The room also contains a fine fresco of the mythological battle between Hercules and the river god Achelous for the hand of Deianeira. The shape-shifting Achelous assumed the form of a dragon and of a bull during the struggle, and only accepted defeat when Hercules tore off one of his horns."

The next image showed a niche where a statue would have stood. "These houses reveal how very religious even the wealthy were in Ephesus. They had statues of the Greek and Roman deities and death masks of their ancestors, whom they would consult on important matters. These people believed whole-heartedly that their ancestors were still alive in Hades."

"One thing for sure," mused Art, "Marissa and I will not be staying in any house that fancy. And where in the world, quite literally, are we going to live? I need to be in the U.S. for the school year and she needs to be here in Istanbul working at the Museum. Should we buy two houses? How will we afford that?" No matter how hard Art tried to focus on his work, those practical questions kept pushing their way to the front of his brain, and he could not exorcise them from his thoughts.

Art was thinking about devoting a whole TV show to the spectacular finds at the Ephesian terrace houses. With bathrooms, kitchens, running water, sunrooms and media rooms, they mirrored the modern wealthy homes of today. Paul surely knew some of the folks that lived in the terrace houses. Perhaps it was one of them who arranged for Paul to lecture in the famous Hall of Tyrannus in Ephesus, a site not yet discovered or dug, but which Art was itching to find. Just when he thought he had managed to crowd out the fear and anxieties about the wedding his cellphone rang. Grabbing it from the little night table next to his chair, he heard Marissa's voice full of stress.

"Arthur, we have a problem. We have an RSVP from two guests who forgot to tell us their names, and we have to have names if they are to be allowed on the cruise for the reception and party afterwards. I need you to see if you recognize the return address—it doesn't match up with anything on my list!"

"Solving your problems will be my sworn duty! I'm betting the two mystery guests are Christy and David Herring—my twin cousins of a sort—it's complicated to me but I'm sure my Mom will be glad to explain it all to you. If all goes well they are on their way by bus from Thessaloniki of all places," replied Art with a flourish putting Ephesus on the back burner once more.

"And you know this because . . ."

"Because David just texted me a couple hours ago!" bragged Art.

Marissa was impressed.

16

EAST VERSUS WEST

WEARING KHAKIS AND A blue polo shirt complete with the Duke insignia, Rev. Dr. James Howell emerged from beyond the barrier at Istanbul airport carrying a Duke travel bag and dragging a suitcase. He smiled broadly when he saw a familiar face—Joyce West who along with a driver had come to collect him at the airport. The wedding now was less than twenty-four hours away, and so Joyce was more than a little glad to see the good reverend.

"My nerves were getting jangled thinking about Art having to find someone at the last minute to perform his wedding, so I am so very glad to see you James," she said with her usual enthusiasm.

"I planned to get here earlier as you know, but duty called. We had two funerals back to back that made me push the flight up to today—and by the way, what day is it? Please tell me the wedding is not today, as I'm too jet-lagged to be coherent."

"No, fortunately you have until tomorrow morning to get your act together," said Joyce. "Today, in fact this afternoon, we will meet with Patriarch Bartholomew. Having the wedding at the Chora Church is a big deal for the Orthodox

Church here, and there's already been media coverage. He wants to make sure you are not going to say anything heretical during the wedding."

"You mean like, the Duke Blue Devils are a better basketball team than the Tar Heels this year?" winked James.

"Something like that," laughed Joyce. After settling into the hotel and having a quick lunch, they rode to the Patriarch's office. The route took them past a relatively new archaeological site—the Harbor of Eleutherio, later known as the Harbor of Theodosius, one of the ports of ancient Constantinople. It is a treasure trove—with sunken ships dating to the tenth century all the way back to artifacts from 6000 B.C.

The driver was chatting away about the fact that the Bosphorus Tunnel Project stumbled upon this amazing site in 2005 but, of course, the excavation significantly delayed the municipal project itself. Finally, after about forty minutes riding in stop and go traffic, they arrived at the Patriarch's compound. Emerging from the taxi, they looked up to see a Greek orthodox priest hastening down the stairs to greet them.

"Welcome, welcome," said Nicholas with a smile. "You must be Mrs. West and Reverend Howell?"

"Yes, forgive us for being a bit tardy; the traffic was all snarled up."

"Do not worry. We have prepared some tea and pastries for you in our reception room just up here to the right. The Patriarch will be joining us shortly."

Neither James nor Joyce was sure about the protocol for this meeting and so they were glad to have some time with Father Nicholas to ask some questions. Father Nicholas also told them that the Patriarch lost one of his closest friends, Father Demetrios, just yesterday. Joyce admitted to having read about it in the morning paper.

"Was it foul play," she immediately asked.

"It may be so, but the police are still investigating." The room suddenly became very quiet.

Without fanfare an elderly man with sparkling eyes entered wearing his ordinary black robe with a large Orthodox cross dangling from his neck. With a smile he came across and greeted Joyce and James who bowed respectfully and then the Patriarch urged them to be seated.

Settling in, Bartholomew said, "Let me first tell you something about the Chora Church and the Orthodox community. We have *not* been allowed to use that building for many centuries and now it is a public museum that the government claims to own. This wedding of Arthur West and Marissa Okur is being allowed by the government only because they are celebrities and it makes for good public relations for the tourist trade. The democratic Turkish government wants to at least appear to be open-minded and fair to Christians.

"But then there is the reality that Orthodox Christians are not allowed to have their own schools and train their own disciples and priests. Our seminary, which resides just off the coast of Istanbul, has been closed for decades. So my hope for this coming wedding is that it will reopen the discussion about the role of Christians in Turkey, and give the Orthodox Church more freedom to practice our religion. Perhaps you saw the recent special on CBS *60 Minutes* about our plight?"

The Patriarch paused to sip some Turkish apple tea, and James responded, "Yes, that report was well done and very enlightening. I honestly did not know you were under such strict constraints. Of course, I read about some of the martyrdoms in eastern Turkey some while back, but I assumed that reflected attitudes of very conservative Muslims like those in Syria and Iran on the Turkish borders."

"That is true, but it seems the problem is now here. Yesterday, I lost a close friend, Father Demetrios. The police are already sure he was murdered for religious reasons. I believe now that he was martyred for his faith. Our situation here is tenuous and perilous even though Constantinople was the epicenter of Christianity for many centuries. In many ways, it still is—my flock ranges worldwide."

"We offer our deep condolences, your Eminence," said Joyce quietly.

"Thank you both. But let us not talk about our troubles. Can you show me the liturgy that will be followed for this wedding?"

Pulling a file from his briefcase, James handed over to the Patriarch the order of service, which in fact was the standard form followed in the Methodist Church. The Patriarch looked it over for several minutes while his guests sipped their tea.

"I see that the wedding will involve the invocation of the Trinity. This pleases me. Your liturgy is much briefer than ours, but I see no objectionable theology here. But, there is one more question I must ask. Are you planning to serve the Eucharist? The Orthodox Church does not recognize the Eucharist as served by Protestants. I would ask you to refrain from 'serving the Lord's Supper' as you call it."

James Howell could see this was important to the Patriarch and so he replied, "Your Holiness we have no desire to offend or cause you headaches, so I will work this out with Arthur and Marissa. We can arrange a very private ceremony if they want to partake of the Eucharist on their wedding day."

"Thank you," he replied with some relief in his voice. "In that case, I can give my official sanction to the service. If only all our ecumenical discussions were this respectful of both parties! During the introductions at the beginning of the wedding, might you mention that you are performing this service not merely with the permission of the Turkish government, but also with the blessing of the Orthodox Church here in Istanbul. That will be a good signal to those present that the Orthodox Church matters in this great city."

"Of course! I will be honored to do that!" said James sincerely.

At this point, Joyce also added, "We would also be blessed if you or one of your representatives could come to the wedding service or any of the festivities!"

The Patriarch smiled, and pondered this request for a moment. "I am tending to the funeral arrangement for Father Demetrios, but I will send Nicholas to represent us. It will be good to have an Orthodox presence at the service."

The Patriarch rose, signaling the end of the meeting. James took the cue and said, "Thank you for your warm welcome and this wonderful apple tea. My congregation will pray that relations between you and the government continue to improve."

Smiling, the Patriarch said, "I never thought there would be a day in my lifetime that a Christian wedding would be held once again in the Chora Church. But I take it as a sign that God can make a way where there seems to be no way. I must leave you now. Please give my blessing to Arthur and Marissa."

Bartholomew turned to leave, but then hesitated, unconsciously tugging on his beard. To Joyce he said, "Mrs. West, would you ask your son to contact me at his earliest convenience about a matter involving his expertise in archaeology? I realize this may need to wait until after the wedding and honeymoon, but tell him it is very important." Handing her a little card with a phone number on it, the Patriarch continued, "If you would just give Professor West this, I will await his call."

"I am sure he would be honored to help in whatever way possible."

Smiling a wry smile, the Patriarch said rather mysteriously, "Well, let us hope so!" And with that he turned and walked out of the room in a slow and stately manner.

James and Joyce chatted with Nicholas for a while. "So have you ever attended a Protestant wedding before?" asked James.

"No, but I'm eager to do so! I'm glad for the opportunity. Please tell Professor West and Dr. Okur to add me to the guest list!"

When they got back, they tracked down Marissa and Art tending to last minute details at the hotel. They were very pleased with all the news from the meeting, except for one issue.

"But we had our hearts set on Holy Communion as a married couple!" complained Marissa.

"I guess I shouldn't be surprised," moaned Art. "Sometimes the Orthodox believers think they are the only ones who practice Christianity properly. I guess this is a case where the East will win out over the West."

"I have a suggestion," said James smiling. "How about we do the communion on the boat immediately after you arrive? Then you can go directly to the reception."

"I guess that's the sort of compromise we must settle for," said a somewhat glum Marissa. "I should be thankful that we have the Patriarch's blessing on our wedding."

"Yes you should! It's a big thing for him to do that and to send his emissary, Father Nicholas," replied James. "The Patriarch is under a lot of stress right now especially since his closest friend, Father Demetrios, was apparently killed yesterday."

"Wasn't another cleric killed only a couple days ago? A Father Donovan, I believe? Two Christians in two days? Could this be the work of an extremist group?" said Art suddenly very worried.

17

FINAL PREPARATIONS

BEING A PART-TIME SECURITY specialist and spy was actually hard work. It did not regularly involve wine, women and song. And certainly not in the case of Sadi Oguz who was happily married with a day job working as a seller of Turkish silk carpets. Sadi had already spoken with Marissa Okur about security—and he also offered his services as carpet expert. She rented a number of beautiful carpets to adorn the boat, the Golden Horn.

On this evening, Sadi was busy donning the plainest clothes a plain clothes man could wear so that he and his security team could keep an eye on the rehearsal at the museum. He had reviewed the latest list of pictures of possible suspects for the murders of the Christian priests, and it was his job to make sure nothing went amiss at the West-Okur wedding. After the recent deaths of the two Christian priests, there could be no slip-ups at this high-profile wedding.

~

The decks of the Golden Horn were fairly gleaming and now the staff was rolling out no less than ten beautiful Turkish carpets, one from each of the major regions in Turkey, and two especially from Cappadocia which had images of churches on them. The chef on board was already preparing the food for over 100 guests invited to tomorrow evening's reception cruise. The menu included all sorts of wonderful Turkish dishes beginning with plates of *meze* (appetizers). The main meal included lentil soup and fresh breads followed by salads, stuffed vegetables (*dolma*), *mücver* (made with zucchini), meat kebabs served skewered, fish and shrimp. Desserts included baklava and rice pudding. The wedding cake itself would be a four-tiered concoction topped with two people on a magic carpet ready to fly away.

~

Christy and David had arrived at midnight the night before. First thing in the morning, they rented scooters from The Magic Carpet—two bright red motorbikes for wending through the streets of Istanbul.

"Whee!" shouted Christy as they went up and down hills, through alleys, and across the Golden Horn on the Galata Bridge. "This really is like a magic carpet ride!" David called out, "Let's head over to the Grand Bazaar for the day." David knew that the bazaar meant food and food was what he wanted. The choices were endless, and with over 3000 shops the day was spent ogling all that Turkey has to offer and dodging thousands of other tourists. The twins spent the day exploring and sampling.

"Hey—look at the time! We promised to be at the rehearsal dinner. And I am not riding this scooter all the way to Chora Church! Let's hustle!" said David emphatically.

"There's a shuttle to the church," promised Christy. Back at the Galata, the two raced up the stairs to the second floor, where Christy managed to hit the shower first. Their halfway decent attire was still wrinkled, but at least they had it. Christy hung up the best they brought for the wedding tomorrow. As they raced down the hall to the elevator, they nearly bumped into a short, dark-haired woman, Meltem Ciftci, Art West's regular tour guide when he worked with Tutku tours owned by Levent Oral. David had been on an earlier trip through parts of Turkey with Cousin Art and knew Mel on sight.

"David—is that really you! You've grown so much," she marveled looking up at the 6'1" hulk who was about to give her a bear hug. Then he introduced Christy who also towered over Meltem.

"I'm waiting for Marissa's parents who are already frazzled at this point. You two should go on and catch the shuttle." Being a tour guide meant Mel was a whiz at getting people to the right place at the right time.

The Okurs were in their late 50s, and Zafer Okur looked very much like the hotel manager he was. His bald head was shining in the lights of the Chora Church, and both he and his wife Zeliha were dressed beyond their normal comfort zone even for the rehearsal. Nonetheless they were every inch the proud and very nervous parents. Zafer would be walking Marissa down the aisle and he was already sweating, not least because he had never attended a Christian wedding.

So the Chora Church saw its first of two invasions of wedding party members and guests. Finally, everyone was all in one place—a miracle in itself. Introductions were made all around. James took on the role of wedding director and soon enough everyone was in their assigned places. They ran through the whole routine twice.

When all was said and done, Art and Marissa stood back and surveyed the assemblage. Yelena was staring at Grayson; Grayson was smiling at Sarah; but Sarah was talking to Hannah, Grace, and Manny about adding Turkish food to the Solomon's Porch menu. The twins, Christy and David, were telling Laura about their adventures in the Grand Bazaar. Joyce was explaining family relations to James Howell, all the while motioning to the cousins to join them. Melody was clinging to Jake. Meltem was keeping Marissa's parents, sister Zehra and cousin Celal mesmerized by extolling the archaeological history of Chora Church in rapid Turkish. Kahlil was standing between two pillars, looking like Samson, trying to fathom why he had been chosen Best Man.

"We are going to have a wonderful wedding," said Art softly to Marissa. And they stood there and kissed, oblivious to the bedlam.

18

HERE COMES THE BRIDE

ART NICKED HIMSELF SHAVING. The gray tuxedo was no problem but the bow tie was another matter. Manny, the tuxedo expert, deftly tied a double Windsor.

Kahlil paced back and forth in the hallway waiting for Art to emerge from his room. No one had ever before asked him to be a best man. The tuxedo made him look all the more like a movie star, although the shoes weren't the most comfortable.

The three friends descended to the lobby. Art had planned to get to the church early—"if you aren't early, you're late" was Art's mantra. He had no intentions of leaving the bride waiting in the vestibule. A flurry of cameras went off as they climbed into their limo. Art barely noticed.

Meanwhile, Marissa's sister was tugging on the zipper of Marissa's wedding dress, trying to get it all the way up to the top. But something was impeding progress. Looking closely she gently released a piece of material caught in the zipper, after which it worked like a charm.

"Hurry up, hurry up! We are already five minutes late for the limo which is waiting outside," moaned Marissa. "I sure hope our musicians have plenty of prelude music," said Marissa to no one in particular.

"They can't start without you," reminded Zehra calmly as she attached the veil to Marissa's head. "Now take your pretty peach flowers here and get thee to the limo!"

Finally, Marissa rode down the elevator and strolled into the lobby where everyone stopped and stared at the creamy lace gown with the peach ribbon. All the bridesmaids were there to greet her, each dressed in a peachy gown with a cream ribbon.

"Does everyone have their posies?" asked Marissa. As if planned, each girl raised her posy bouquet in salute.

As she walked out the front door of the hotel, cameras again went off—the Turkish paparazzi had arrived in force along with the legitimate local papers. One by one the ladies stuffed themselves into the stretch limo. "Make it snappy," said Marissa to the driver, "I have a date with destiny!"

"Strange," said Laura Joyce. "I thought you were marrying my brother Art."

~

The string quartet had been playing for thirty minutes but their instructions were quite clear—just keep playing. The first ones to arrive at the church were Melody, Jake and Joyce who had vowed to never be late for anything except her own funeral! The music was much to Joyce's taste, being the piano teacher she was. A nice selection of Bach, Vivaldi, Telemann and Beethoven filled the vaulted nave. Jake continued to seat the groom's guests; and Manny acted as usher to seat the bride's guests. Each guest immediately gazed up at the incredible Christian art hovering overhead, as if the saints and apostles and angels were all attending this wedding and wishing it well.

When all were seated, Joyce West and Zeliha Okur went down the aisle to the altar upon which were two lit candles in the middle and one unlit candle on each side of them. They each took one of the lit candles and together lit the candle on the left side to signal the union of two families. No, only the candle on the right remained unlit.

James Howell then signaled Art and Kahlil to come forward and join him in front of the altar. To everyone's surprise a musician from the jazz

 group began playing Purcell's Trumpet Voluntary. The horn's notes echoed throughout the hall swirling up into the various mini-domes above and filling the room with a rich warm sound as the bridesmaids began their march down to the front. Laura Joyce

was the first, followed by Meltem, and then Marissa's first cousin, Celal. Finally, Zehra entered as the Maid of Honor.

The church went quiet. Then the strains of Mussorgsky's 'The Great Gate of Kiev' from 'Pictures at an Exhibition' grandly filled the Chora Church. Marissa began to walk down the aisle on the arm of her father. Art was transfixed. When Marissa glided to Art's side, James Howell looked out at everyone and began the ceremony.

"Dearly Beloved, we are gathered here today in the sight of God and this company to join in holy matrimony this couple—Arthur James West and Marissa Okur. Marriage is an honorable estate, instituted of God. It is, therefore, not to be entered into unadvisedly, but reverently, discreetly, and in the fear of God. Into this holy estate these two persons come now to be joined.

"Let us pray. Heavenly Father, love has been your richest and greatest gift to the world. Love between a man and woman that matures into marriage is one of your most beautiful types of loves. Today we celebrate that love. May your blessing be on this wedding. Protect, guide, and bless Arthur and Marissa in their marriage. Surround them and us with your love now and always. Jesus once blessed the wedding at Cana with both his presence and a miracle and we ask for his blessing on and his presence at this wedding as well, Amen."

"Who gives this woman to be married to this man?"

"Marissa's mother and I do," said Mr. Okur who squeezed his daughter's hand before turning it over to Art.

The lead singer of the jazz band stepped out with a Spanish guitar to sing Paul Stookey's classic wedding song, 'There is Love'.

James then continued. "Arthur do you take Marissa to be your wedded wife, and in the presence of God and these witnesses do you vow that you will do everything in your power to make your love for her a growing part of your life? Will you continue to strengthen it from day to day and week to week with your best resources? Will you stand by her in sickness or in health, in poverty or in wealth, and will you shun all others and keep yourself to her alone as long as you both shall live?"

Art proudly said, "I will," and Marissa soon echoed the sentiment with her vows.

James then led them in the exchange of rings which Kahlil carefully produced.

"The wedding ring is a symbol of eternity. It is an outward sign of an inward and spiritual bond that unites two hearts in endless love. And now as a token of your love and of your deep desire to be forever united in heart and soul, you Arthur may place a ring on the finger of your bride." Art then said: "In the sight of God and these witnesses I give you this ring as a symbol of my love and faithfulness to you, now and forever." Marissa repeated the liturgy. Art and Marissa gazed at the perfectly fitting rings with a sense of amazement.

There was still one unlit candle on the altar. Art and Marissa walked over and gently lifted the two central candles and used them to light the candle on the right. Then they returned.

James explained, "The two central candles were lighted to represent your separate lives. They are two distinct lights, each capable of going their separate ways. Your mothers lit the candle on the left to join the families. Now you have joined the central candles into one light representing your marriage. From now on your thoughts shall be for each other rather than for your individual selves. Your plans shall be mutual, your joys and sorrows shall be shared. May the radiance of this one light be a testimony of your unity in the Lord."

James then faced the congregation and said to all, "Inasmuch as Arthur and Marissa have consented together in holy wedlock, and have witnessed the same before God and these witnesses, and have pledged their faithfulness each to the other, and have pledged the same by the giving and receiving each of a ring, by the authority invested in me as a minister of the gospel, I pronounce that they are husband and wife together, in the

threefold name of God the Father, Son, and Holy Spirit. Those that God has joined together let no one put asunder."

James then said to the congregation, "And now the moment you've all been waiting for. Art, you may kiss your forever bride." Art lifted the transparent veil, gently took Marissa's face in his hands and kissed her. As he did so he happened to look over and above Marissa's shoulder and there in the dome above was an angel, his hand raised in the sign of peace and blessing! God's love must have really been shining down on us today, thought Art.

"Ladies and gentleman I am proud to present to you Mr. and Mrs. West." At this point loud applause broke out in the church on both sides of the aisle, and the recessional music began with Art striding down the aisle with Marissa on his arm beaming at one and all. They had done it!

Sadi Oguz was seated with Father Nicholas. "It was a beautiful ceremony," said Sadi to the Father. "What did you think?"

"It was not done according to the Greek Orthodox liturgy for a wedding but still it had its beautiful moments. I especially appreciated the vows. Life-long marriage is too rare a thing these days."

Sadi replied, "How right you are. When I go to weddings I constantly thank Allah that I have had a good wife and a good marriage for more than thirty years now."

Behind them in the next row Manny was saying to Grace, "Boy was that different from our wedding. Look at the *chuppah* over their heads— gold painted no less," he remarked staring up at the domes.

Grace agreed, "Well, darling, at least we now have a good roof over our head, even if our wedding was in a roofless synagogue."[1]

Yelena said, "I want a pretty dress like that someday!"

By now the congregation had mostly exited the church and the press and paparazzi got off a few shots from behind a barrier before the bridal party slipped back in for formal pictures. The rest of the guests ran the gauntlet and headed to the party boat, the Golden Horn. The police were there to manage the traffic.

But across the courtyard from the entrance to the church, standing next to a gift shop was a small man with a cigarette in his hand watching all that transpired. As the limo carrying Art and Marissa drove by, he flicked his cigarette ash in the car's direction and murmured, "Ashes to ashes, dust to dust." It was Aziz.

1. This story is told in the third Art West adventure *Papias and the Mysterious Menorah*.

19

ON THE GOLDEN HORN

Marissa and Art sat in the back of the limo holding hands in stunned silence. They were in a fog of euphoria, exhaustion, and exhilaration. Marissa put her head on Art's shoulder and snuggled in for the remainder of the ride. The usually verbal Art was quiet as a church mouse, content to let everything just soak into his heart and mind, and to settle back down to a lower adrenaline level.

When he finally opened his mouth, all he could say was, "I'm glad we got through that without major foul ups. My smile was sort of frozen in place for those photos."

"Me too," said a small voice beside him. "I thought the service was Christian enough, without offending the non-Christians. I think we struck the right balance. It will be interesting to get feedback from my parents, however."

"Agreed! So are you ready for Round 2?" Marissa nodded and they both drifted back into their own thoughts about the wedding and reception.

Suddenly the sound of a loud horn jolted them back to the present. The Golden Horn, a beautiful cruise boat with two decks, gleaming in the late afternoon sun was moored and ready for them.

As he and Marissa walked briskly up the breezeway, they were greeted by the captain, a tall thin man with grey hair named Taner Oral. "You wouldn't be any relation to Levent Oral would you?" asked Art. Levent owned Tutku tours, based in Izmir, and had long been Art's choice when planning his Middle Eastern tours.

"Why yes," said a surprised Taner, "he is my first cousin! And I see that Meltem is one of your bridesmaids. Is that not so Mrs. West!"

Marissa responded. "Captain, I think you are the first to call me Mrs. West! And yes, Meltem is a bridesmaid! Art, Levent was at the wedding and will certainly be here for the reception. I thought you knew!"

"I'm sure I did, but to be honest, it's all a blur!" laughed Art.

The captain continued, "We have carefully noted the arrival of all your guests. My assistant Cacelia is in charge of checking off names. And Sadi Oguz is already on board checking the security. I might add that his man Mehmet over there is in charge of any gate crashers. Security is tight, I promise."

Taner escorted the newlyweds down some narrow stairs to their quarters so that they could freshen up before entering the reception. For a few moments they were actually alone together and took full advantage of the time to kiss in private until Marissa said, "The good reverend is probably waiting for us in the captain's quarters. He has set up Holy Communion."

Art was impressed by how insistent Marissa had been about having communion together. They knelt before the makeshift altar, and James gave them the fresh pita bread while saying the words, "This is my body broken for you." He handed them a cup of Turkish port wine to share and said, "This is my blood shed for you." Both Art and Marissa were so moved by the moment that large tears of joy streamed down their faces. There was something intimate and special about this quiet moment in which they could be still and recognize the need for Christ at the center of their relationship.

Rising, they left the cabin and Art quipped, "Time to face the music. Pretty soon everyone is going to know, I can't dance a lick!"

Marissa just giggled and said, "What does it matter. You should be too giddy in love to care how silly you look. I know I am."

More pictures were taken on deck, which took some time because Marissa's now auburn hair kept blowing in the wind. And more pictures were taken in the reception area especially of Art and Marissa dancing their first dance as Miss Demir sang Journey's "Faithfully." And there were pictures of the amazing buffet dinner and the formal cake-cutting ceremony.

The dancing lasted long into the evening as the Golden Horn cruised up and down the Turkish waterways. They passed mosques, Ottoman palaces, and the Maiden's Tower, made famous in the James Bond movie,

"From Russia with Love." Everyone seemed to be having a fabulous time, and after enough local Turkish wine even Art was prompted to get up on the dance floor with Marissa. The slow dance to "Faithfully" had produced applause, but Art's attempt at some 70s style rock and roll dancing produced loud laughs from various friends. Art frankly did not care. Nothing was going to steal his joy on this day.

Art watched Christy and David dance all the fast ones with each other, and all the slow ones with various other guests. Joyce West got on the floor for a slow dance with Art, Kahlil, and even Mr. Okur. Being secular Muslims there was no stigma in touching a woman that was not one's wife. The Cohens kept everyone entertained with stories about the gaffs at their own wedding. Grayson got up enough courage to dance with Sarah, but everyone enjoyed watching him dance with little Yelena. Melody's arms could barely reach Jake's neck, but they slow danced all night despite what the music demanded. Laura and Hannah were game to try some Turkish dances led by some of Marissa's cousins. Levent, Mel and Art had an impromptu business meeting to seal the deal on a tour to be led by both Art and Marissa.

20

HONEYMOON BOUND

FINALLY, IT WAS TIME to change into something more comfortable for the eventual getaway. This produced an awkward moment with the couple alone in their guest room when Marissa said, "How about unzipping me?" And when Art obliged he simply stood there staring at his beautiful bride who proceeded to take almost everything off without any hesitation at all.

"I've seen you in a bikini—but somehow this is different," laughed Art nervously.

Marissa countered, "Now it's time for you to get into something more comfortable." Feeling a bit sheepish, Art turned around and took off his clothes, but just when he had nothing on but his underwear, he felt warm arms wrapping around him. He slowly turned and began to kiss Marissa passionately. His body responded to the moment.

Marissa laughed and said, "It's good to know you like me, because you're stuck with me now, but we need to get back to the reception! Sorry to get your hopes up!"

Quickly getting dressed, they returned to the reception hall and were met again with cheers from one and all. Art was sporting a tan jacket and sport shirt, and Marissa a blue halter-top summer dress. Slowly, patiently they went around from table to table and couple to couple greeting everyone and accepting congratulations. At one point they congratulated Grayson on completing his degree, and said they regretted missing graduation day.

"Hey, don't worry, just be happy. A honeymoon is a great excuse for missing my grad day," said Grayson with a big smile. "Make it a good one!" he added and then blushed.

Just then, Kahlil boomed out, "It's time for the big toast! To Art and Marissa, may they always be in love as much as they are today!"

"Here, here!" cried the guests in unison.

"Even when they are on a hot, sweaty dig in the middle of nowhere," chimed in Grayson.

"Here, here!" cried the guests in unison.

And as the bubbly was consumed and the sun slowly sank on the Wests as they sailed the Bosphorus, it would have been hard to imagine a more joyful occasion.

Eventually, all good things must come to an end. At 9 PM, the boat pulled slowly to the dock. A taxi was waiting to take Art and Marissa to the Pera Palace Hotel—which Laura personally recommended after her two-day romantic stay.

For a while they sat side-by-side on their private balcony with a glass of champagne, watching the moon rise over Istanbul. They were certainly tired, but Art put his right arm around Marissa, and she turned and gave

him a long lingering kiss. On impulse, he picked her up, carried her to the bed and gently set her down. When love comes to full expression, not even the weariness of the flesh can get in the way.

The next morning, after a late, private brunch in their room, they took the short flight to Izmir, picked up a rental car, and drove the 80 km (50 miles) slowly south along the coast to the port of Kushadasi. They finally arrived in the late afternoon.

When Art got out of the car, he could smell the sea air. The Sea Pines stands right on the crest of a hill overlooking the bay where the cruise boats dock. Hearing the sea birds above, Art remarked, "The gulls are serenading us on our first day together."

"I just hope they don't wake us up in the morning. By the way, alarm clocks are banished on this honeymoon," replied Marissa as they reached the check-in desk.

"Art West and his wife Marissa," said Art proudly.

"Yes!" beamed the man behind the counter, "We've been expecting you. The honeymoon suite is ready, and you will find a complimentary bottle of champagne on ice. But I've also included one of our best local Sevilen wines, a sauvignon." Handing them their room keys, he said, "Enjoy!"

"We will!" both Art and Marissa said in unison.

The thing about newly married couples is that they tend to be oblivious to everything and everyone else, and Art and Marissa were no different. When they got into their taxi at the Golden Horn, they had not noticed the man who followed them to the Pera Palace Hotel and next day to the airport. So self-absorbed were they that they paid no attention to anything or anyone that did not absolutely demand their attention, such as the man next to them buying a ticket to Izmir.

The phrase "love is blind" can have a variety of meanings and in this case it meant that Art and Marissa had tunnel vision. They most certainly did not notice the small Turkish man who followed them down the concourse to their plane, nor did they pay any attention to the man that rented a car and followed them to Kushadasi. And the next day when they visited the terrace houses at Ephesus, well he was just one of hundreds of tourists.

21

THE TOURISTS SCATTER

AFTER THE EUPHORIA OF the wedding, Joyce West found herself a little sad and out of sorts, and she was not at all sure why. True, the wedding had gone smoothly, and true the reception had been spectacular, but she had a feeling of dread, a feeling that something bad might happen, and she was not sure why. And she was just sad that she couldn't talk longer with Kahlil and Grace and Manny and Art's other various friends to ask them about their lives. She thrived on hearing other's life stories.

True she enjoyed dancing with Kahlil and others at the reception. True she relished all the Turkish food and drink. True she loved watching Art and Marissa cut the cake and dance their slow dance of joy and love. The truth was she was feeling a little lonely. She was glad that Art finally had someone in his life, but it reminded her that she no longer did. Thank goodness for her houseguest Jake Arafat, but it looked like he was soon going to get married as well! Then all of sudden she remembered something she had completely forgotten to do—give the Patriarch's card and phone number to Art! Like a bolt of lightning the oversight struck her, though it was understandable she would forget in the midst of all the excitement.

She would have to get in touch with Art and was tempted to call him immediately on his cell phone. But, for a change, she resisted the temptation especially when Laura came into her room. Joyce looked at Laura quizzically.

Laura raised her eyebrows. "Don't you remember we are spending the day with Jake, Melody, and the twins? I sure want to see Hagia Sophia! And the Topkapi Palace! We have a private day-tour set up for the six of us! If you're up to it, you can join me for a museum tour tomorrow."

"Yes, of course, dear," said Joyce with less than her usual enthusiasm. "What about Reverend Howell?"

"Remember? He told us at breakfast that he's spending the day with Levent to plan a tour next year for Myers Park Church. You should go—on the tour that is!"

"I can't get beyond today!" moaned Joyce.

The Cohens made sure that Hannah, Kahlil, Grayson, and Sarah would have a ride back to Jerusalem as soon as they finished spending a few days sightseeing. They had only to give their pilot a day's notice of their departure. Yelena enjoyed seeing the Topkapi Palace but in the evening they all packed their bags and headed to the plane for a flight to Antalya on the Turkish Riviera. The next morning found them at the ancient city of Aspendos with its remarkably preserved Roman theater, located 25 miles east of Antalya.

Grace thought the wedding had gone exceptionally well, and the security was very unobtrusive. At one point in the reception pictures of Art and Marissa from their younger days appeared magically on a screen for all to see. Grace enjoyed seeing Art blush at the sight of a 70s picture of him in a tie-dyed, t-shirt and bell bottoms. His hair was thicker and a lot longer then. While mulling the wedding over, Grace turned to her husband.

"Manny honey, I think we have to take more time to see the world," mused Grace as she stared up at the sharp incline at which the seats at the Aspendos Theater were pitched. "We've been living too much of a sheltered existence, too buried in our own little work lives in Israel. Isn't it about time we expanded our horizons? I mean look at this theater. This makes the theater in Caesarea Maritima, even as restored as it is, look shabby. If this theater exists and I never had any idea it was this impressive, I'm thinking there are a lot of other sites we have missed, but shouldn't have."

Manny was trying not to get a huge crick in his neck looking up. He could envision a lot more sight-seeing trips, and this produced a sigh. This was the price he paid for marrying a woman who loved antiquity and antiquities. "Yes dear. Doubtless you are right." Just then Grace's cellphone went off.

"Hello? Yes, this is Grace Levine, how can I help?" After a long explanation from the other end, she cried, "They've found what? Well, no, I certainly won't believe it until I see the hard evidence. Are you sure it's not just another copy of the Gospel of Thomas? You're certain? And it's in Aramaic? When I get back to Jerusalem I will be glad to have a look." Hanging up, Grace was a silent for a moment.

"I guess we'd better head back to Tel Aviv sooner rather than later. That was Sammy Cohen at the IAA. Someone claims to have found Q?!"

"The letter?"

"More than one letter, dear. Q is the short name for the earliest collection of Jesus' sayings, predating the Gospels. Apparently an Aramaic document has been found buried in Capernaum, right next to where we had our wedding no less. Sammy says it could well be the Q document."

"Maybe one of our more mischievous wedding guests planted a fake there last year to test how good an epigrapher you really are!" said Manny with a devilish grin.

"Maybe you had it planted to make sure we wouldn't stay away from all your work in Tel Aviv for too long," Grace rebutted.

"Surely not," said Manny with a mock wounded look. "Would I do that?"

Grace punched him in the bicep and said, "Let's stay another day or two here and enjoy the scenery. I promised Yelena we would take her to see the Whirling Dervish show tonight, to say nothing of the water park at Konyaalti Beach. The Q documents have been a mystery for a long time—a day or two won't matter. But this isn't the long vacation I envisioned. I guess the balloon ride in Cappadocia will have to wait until next time."

22

THE FAR EAST OF TURKEY

AFTER TWO HONEYMOON NIGHTS in Kushadasi, Art and Marissa drove back to Izmir for a two-hour direct flight to Gaziantep in eastern Turkey. Both had turned off their cellphones and their internal alarm systems as well. Once again, the same man booked himself on the same flight they were taking from Izmir, but no one noticed.

Art and Marissa arrived in Gaziantep, a city of over a million people in time to check into their hotel and visit the newly opened Zeugma Mosaic Museum, the world's largest museum devoted to ancient mosaics.

Early the next morning they drove about 90 miles north in their rental car to Sanliurfa (or just Urfa to the locals) to see the mosque which marks the grotto or cave site where, according to Islamic tradition, Abraham the Prophet was born. They continued northward for about 2 hours to Mt. Nemrut, an artificial mountain featuring two temples each with colossal statues over 2000 years old.

Marissa decided to paraphrase some information from the guidebook about this famous mountain while Art drove.

"Antiochus the First was one interesting Hellenistic ruler, whose reign lasted from 281—261 B.C.," said Marissa. "His father, King Mithridates, was a direct descendent of the most famous King of Persia, Darius I, also known as Darius the Great, who was in turn the descendent by marriage of Cyrus the Persian. He's the good guy who set Judean Jews free in about 525 B.C. and allowed them to return to Jerusalem."

Perched on top of Mt. Nimrut, Antiochus' own personal Mount Olympus, not to mention his burial mound, were statues that Art had always wanted to see and Marissa had not seen in many years. Marissa continued the explanation. "There are statues of both Greek and Persian deities reflecting Antiochus' ancestry, but there are also statues of Antiochus and his own family. Plus, we have stone friezes, one of which depicts Antiochus in what looks like celestial pajamas with crescent moons all over them! He's wearing a fashionable pointy hat as well, and could be mistaken for Merlin the magician. On top of the mount, there is a famous stele written in the most impressive and hyperbolic Asiatic rhetoric imaginable with sentences that go on and on without end. But you need to know that the phrases are a form of Greek rhetoric found in the New Testament in letters like Ephesians."

The car could only go so far up the steep incline. Art and Marissa had to park below the café /tourist shop and walk the remaining half mile up to the top of Mt. Nemrut. The wind was blowing fiercely on this June day, but the sky was clear and one could see for miles from this peak.

Stopping in front of the lion (*Oguz* in Turkish), Art noticed a small man with a moustache wandering around the site quite a distance off but there were few other tourists about on this hot day.

Later, he asked the man to take their picture, explaining that they were on their honeymoon. He readily obliged, smiling all the while. As he left, he said, "See you later!" Art thought his remark was rather odd. That night Aziz shaved off his scraggly beard and his famous moustache.

23

POT BELLY HILL

THEIR STAY IN THE Shanli Urfa Palace (Shanli meaning "beautiful"), a hotel carved out of a sheer rock cliff, had been pleasant. Art dreamed he single-handedly moved large stone heads in an attempt to find the tomb of Antiochus. Art frantically vowed that he would leave no stone unturned until he found the ancient ruler's burial site. He awoke too soon to accomplish his goal.

Today they would drive the ten miles to Göbeckli Tepe, which means Pot Belly Hill, one of the more spectacular finds in any of the lands of the Bible, and the oldest religious site by far. This would be a first for both Art and Marissa.

Marissa was munching on an apple and reading a technical report which began with a recreation drawing of the site's oldest layers dating back

to nearly 10,000 BC.

"Göbekli Tepe is the oldest human-made place of worship yet discovered. Until excavations began in 1993, a complex on this scale was not thought possible for a community so ancient. The layers suggest civilization back to perhaps 10,000 B.C. The oldest occupation layer contains pillars linked by coarsely built walls to form circular or oval structures. So far, four such buildings, with diameters between ten and thirty meters have been uncovered. Geophysical surveys indicate the existence of sixteen additional structures."

Marissa had to stop reading as she tended to get carsick pretty quickly. "You remember that Klaus Schmidt started the dig in '93 after being convinced that the mound was prehistoric. When he said 'first came the temple and then the city' he really opened up a can of worms. If he's right, and I think he is, then religion was there at the beginning. The theory that civilization came first, and religion much later, simply doesn't work. Human beings seem to be inherently religious!"

Art smiled at his beautiful bride and said, "And guess what? The writers of the Bible could have said, 'I told you so.' The Bible begins with the story of human beings created in God's image and meant for relationship with God, meant for worship, and Göbeckli Tepe is a worship site. And it's a worship site near one of those rivers of Eden, the Euphrates. In fact it's between the Euphrates and the Tigris. I am wondering just how far this site could be from ancient Eden."

The glow of wedded bliss had not worn off, and the couple remained pretty much oblivious to all that was going on around them, including the fact that a small gray car followed them all the way from Urfa and stopped about a hundred yards behind where the couple had parked to go and visit the site. As they walked up the crest of the hill to the entrance to the dig they were met almost immediately by Dr. Klaus Schmidt himself. Meltem, who knew the famous German archaeologist, had called ahead so the Wests could get a proper tour of the site.

"Welcome to our little world called Gö-beckli Tepe!" said Klaus with a big smile. He was a well-tanned German wearing the ever-present white head covering to protect himself from the hot sun.

"I am delighted to be able to show you around our site, and would value your opinion of what the relevance of this site might be for a biblical archaeologist."

"We're here to learn, but if anything comes to mind, I will certainly share it. On our way we were discussing that we seem to have clear evidence that in the Stone Age if not before, human beings were profoundly religious creatures. That in itself is enormously significant."

"Quite so," said Klaus beaming. "What is interesting but odd about this site is that it seems to be something of a worship center, by which I mean a complex of circular or rectangular structures all of which had something to do with sacrifice."

"What do you make of all the carved reliefs of animals, many of them not your typical choice for sacrifice?" asked Marissa.

"That is quite puzzling, isn't it? On the one hand I don't think we are dealing with the first zoo here, but on the other hand, many of these monoliths have both carvings of animals and of uplifted hands."

Marissa continued. "The motif of uplifted hands is a very ancient prayer gesture mentioned in the Bible and other ancient near eastern sources. So I think there is no escaping the religious connotations of this site. The animals were surely votive offerings to some deity. I read your detailed article, 'Zuerst kam der Tempel, dann die Stadt,' and I agree with the thesis. Human beings have always been inherently religious, indeed burial rites are often the first sign we find of a human presence. And from a biblical point of view there is a ready explanation—we were all created as religious beings, created in the image of God and meant for relationship with the divine."

Art had a question. "But what do you make of the lack of human iconography here, with the exception being the naked woman icon?"

Klaus laughed. "We have many questions, but not enough answers! I don't know what to make of the naked woman statue. Is she a goddess? A sacrifice? A sacrificer? And here are some of my other questions. What pushes the Neolithic human to create such a monumental sacred complex? What tools did the builders of the temples use to erect up to 70-ton colossal blocks? Could the monumental pillars and animal carvings be the mysterious symbols of a code waiting to be cracked for 12,000 years?"

Marissa's mouth dropped. "You are thinking in grand terms! But I have a few simpler questions of my own. Was this site actually buried under a mountain of sand, as reported? If so, do you think it was buried by humans or by some ancient flood? And that leads to a question about the biblical flood story. Mt. Ararat isn't far from here. Do you suppose these are images of antediluvian creatures, some of which ended up in an ark, and some of which were drowned in the flood that also covered this site?"

"Wow!" said Klaus. "You must have been watching that recent History Channel special. Of course I have no answer to those questions either. There could be a connection between the biblical flood and our site here."

Art added, "Well, almost all these ancient cultures had a saga about an ancient flood. There's the Epic of Gilgamesh that is perhaps the closest parallel to the biblical story. Even if one is not persuaded that the Bible records straight history, when there are various lines of evidence all pointing to a large ancient flood in the Mediterranean region, including geological evidence, we must take them seriously!"

"You're right," said Klaus. Follow me over to those standing stones— they weigh tons! What sort of tools did these ancients have to carve such stones? These people didn't even have pottery, much less metal tools!!"

After a short hike and a bottle of cold water, they arrived at a remarkable stone.

"Here is one of the first stones uncovered, and by the way this story starts rather like the Dead Sea Scrolls story. A Kurdish farmer, out in his field, discovers one of these monoliths. We are not sure what to make of the long 45 degree angled line over that animal figure."

"And here we have a boar or wart hog at the bottom, and perhaps camels on the top. Keep in mind that these stones pre-date Stonehenge by about 6,000 years and the pyramids by 3,000 or so years."

Walking up to the top of a hill, the three archaeologists looked down from above on this remarkable site. "Notice how perfectly formed these stones are, how symetrical and straight. At a minimum we know that some sort of advanced civilization is much older than we imagined it to be. And Professor West I must ask you a delicate question. Do you think the Bible suggests that the world is only 6,000—10,000 years old?"

"No!" replied Art firmly. "That sort of calculation comes from adding up genealogical records with a starting point at the Exodus in say 1290 B.C. but the fly in that ointment is that the genealogies are hardly complete. They are selective in character. The Bible tells us nothing about the age of the earth or for that matter the age of human civilization, despite the speculation of many Bible lovers and even a few scholars through the ages."

The next stone that Marissa and Art saw produced a gasp. "Look at the detail in this stone. We seem to have some sort of scorpion and a vulture and an ibis perhaps. Could those be baskets on top?' asked Art.

"Yes, they look somethng like baskets, or could they be dwelling places?" mused Klaus.

Marissa suggested, "Perhaps they are baskets for bread offerings to the deity. Oh, look, here is the statue of the woman! She is pretty typical. We have some like this in the Istanbul Museum from a later period in time. It's usually an image of some fertility goddess."

Then Klaus showed them the statue of a man. "He seems to be wearing some sort of collared garment, but I believe he will remain a mystery for some time."

"I'm guessing it will take lifetimes. Göbeckli Tepe will be designated a UNESCO World Heritage Site, I presume," said Art hopefully.

"Yes, it's just a matter of paperwork and patience," replied Klaus laughing.

Before they knew it, four hours had gone by and Klaus had enjoyed showing Art and Marissa the highlights for an extended period of time. It was already late afternoon, and the couple sensed that Klaus needed to get back to the enormous tasks at hand (less than 15% of the site is so far uncovered) so they bid him farewell and began heading back down the tiny single lane road towards Urfa. They did not notice that their right rear tire had a slow leak. When the tire went entirely flat, they were still a couple of miles outside of Urfa.

Pulling up behind them was a small man in a gray car. He hopped out of his car and headed over to the West's vehicle.

24

RIGHT ON Q

GRACE LEVINE WAS A highly regarded expert in ancient epigraphy, especially when it came to Aramaic inscriptions. She was in frequent demand from the media for a whole host of reasons, and in this case it was because this new Q document was not, as one might expect, in Greek, but rather it had the sayings of Jesus in his native tongue of Aramaic. Grace was chomping at the bit to see the original manuscript and to get a clear detailed photocopy so she could begin to analyze it. But for now she had to abide her soul in patience as she would not get to see the manuscript until the private, after-hours meeting at 6 PM at the Israeli Antiquities Authorities (IAA). This was precisely the sort of ground-breaking project that she loved to sink her teeth into. At the moment she was on the phone with Rami Arav who had been in charge of the digs at Bethsaida and Capernaum where the scroll was found not 100 yards from the famous House of Peter.

Something had jogged Grace's memory about Art West's recent discoveries in Hierapolis. What was it that Papias of Hierapolis said in the second century about the Gospel of Matthew? Sitting in her office at Hebrew University and munching on a bagel with cream cheese, she found what she was looking for online.

"Here it is, just one line: 'Matthew put together the oracles [of the Lord] in the Hebrew language, and each one interpreted them as best he could.'" As Grace knew, the term Hebrew could just as well refer to Aramaic, as it would be all the same to someone like Papias who probably didn't read Semitic languages. But the interesting bit here was the word *logia*—words or oracles. Nothing here about a Gospel or a memoir like Papias' comments on Mark. No, it says Matthew put together the oracles—Jesus sayings—in a Semitic language. And this jogged yet a further memory of a conversation with Art.

Art maintained that the more likely origin for the Gospel of Matthew was Capernaum not Antioch, the latter being the majority opinion. He also felt that this was a Gospel written for Jewish Christians living in close contact with non-Christian Jews. Capernaum certainly fit the bill on that point. So maybe Matthew, the literate tax collector, 1) obtained a copy of Mark's Gospel; 2) made a collection of Jesus' sayings in Aramaic; and 3) added unique traditions he himself had discovered through talking with eyewitnesses! Papias would seem to be talking about the the second of these three source documents. What Grace wanted to know is which version of the sayings of Jesus were in this so-called Q scroll. Would it be more like Luke's version, or more like Matthew's? Most Q scholars tended to think Luke reflected the earlier version of these sayings, but Art West usually disagreed, saying the more Jewish form of the sayings was in Matthew. Maybe he's right!

Suddenly the phone rang, startling Grace out of her reverie.

"Hi Grace, it's Sarah. I'm still in Istanbul. Where are you?"

"We flew back this morning even though we planned to stay longer and go to Cappadocia. If you've got the time you should go. Just have our pilot take you out there. But I had to come back and I'm already at the office. Something really big has come up. Tonight I've got to deal with the IAA and then I have an interview with *Ha'Aretz* after that. You can read about it in the papers!"

"The life of a media star is hard to bear," teased Sarah. "We mere mortals simply bask in your glow!"

"Alright, alright! When will you be back, girlfriend?"

"I'm thinking Sunday—thanks for the jet rides, by the way. Anyway, you and I should get together next week for lunch at Solomon's Porch. I didn't get to talk to you much after the wedding. And we need to visit Samuel! Hannah has turned into the über-Mom she always wanted to be."

Sarah could have rattled on for a while, but Grace was pressed for time. "Just call me when you get back, Sarah! I promise I'll make the time, if you promise to go to Cappadocia on my behalf!"

"Such a deal I can't refuse! Now get back to work!" scolded Sarah before she hung up.

Grace wanted to call Rami Arav and talk to him about the document's history. The call took several tries, but finally he was able to answer his cell phone. "*Shalom*, who is calling?" said Rami from his trailer office at the Bethsaida dig site.

"*Alechum shalom*, Rami. It's Grace in Jerusalem. Don't you have caller ID? Anyway, I need you to tell me all the essentials about this so-called Q scroll or Q document or Jesus scroll or whatever we finally decide to call it! I need some background—when, where and by whom was it discovered?"

Grace could hear chuckling at the other end of the phone. "You get right to the point, don't you? The when is about a month ago—I can get you the exact date from our log entries. And I'm proud to say that my understudy, Elena Horowitz, was supervising the dig that day and did a superb job securing the site. It awaits your inspection anytime you want to make a visit. As for the where, it was found about 50 meters from the lake and about 30 meters from the synagogue and only 90 meters from the Peter House. And yes, it was found in the ground. We were excavating a new house and found two things. First, a cache of first century coins, and secondly the document in a decayed leather container. Thank goodness for the container or else we would probably have no scroll, which is in pretty good shape considering. We haven't figured out if there's a connection between the coins and the document though."

"Here's an idea to try out. Let's suppose you've dug up the house of a tax collector. Now this tax collector might have lots of coins and be literate enough to keep records and maybe even write the scroll!"

Ravi took a deep breath. "Now that's an interesting notion. Do you actually have someone in particular in mind?"

Grace laughed, "Perhaps you've heard of Matthew of Capernaum, one of the original disciples of Jesus?"

"Holy parchments! You think we may have hit the motherlode here? You think maybe we found one of the source documents for Matthew's Gospel?"

"Can't say whether this is plausible or not until I see this now famous document. I will get to that this afternoon. I'll let you know if it looks like first century Aramaic script. We'll talk about the rest later. Got to go now!"

"Looking forward to it! Ciao!"

Grace leaned back in her chair until it nearly fell over backwards. She sighed and said, "If only it were true. Imagine having the original words of Jesus in Matthew's own hand!" The idea sent excited chills up and down her spine.

25

THE GOOD SAMARITAN

ART WEST WAS ALREADY getting the full-sized spare tire out of the back of their rented car. "Well it could be worse, honey. We might have had to deal with a balloon tire or a tow truck."

"Ha! You think we have tow trucks everywhere for rent here in Turkey? You must be joking." Marissa was standing over Art as he was jacking up the back of the little car.

Aziz had been standing quietly about ten feet from the car, and now approached. "Having car trouble? Can I assist you in any way?"

"No, I think we have it under control now," said Marissa turning to face Aziz and fanning herself with a travel brochure she found in the rental car. The temperature was well over ninety in this southeastern corner of Turkey where the climate was semi-arid.

"But perhaps there is something I can do. I have cold beverages in my car. Would that help?"

"Now you're talking, as long as its not Ayran. Art won't touch that native yogurt drink even if it is quite cold," explained Marissa a bit testily considering the man was only trying to help.

The nuts on the tire were proving more difficult to budge than Art had expected as they were somewhat rusted out. And now Art was sweating profusely as he tugged and pulled and twisted the socket wrench to get the nuts off the screws holding the tire in place. Art glanced over at Aziz who quickly turned to go back to his car. He returned with two cold drinks, each in soft drink cans, and each with the tops already popped.

"Here you go pretty lady. I am sorry for your trouble, but I must move along now." Handing over the drinks Aziz bowed.

"*Teşekkür ederim* [thank you]," said Marissa as the man walked off.

Returning to Art, she said, "It's always nice to find a good Samaritan on the side of a road in Turkey. Here, have a cold drink. Not sure what it is, but it's definitely cold. Probably a Turka Cola. I'll try a bit but I'd rather get some water out of the trunk."

Art took the cold can and guzzled the cola down almost in one gulp. Wiping his mouth with the back of his hand he said, "That hit the spot. I liked it."

Marissa was not a big fan of colas, preferring cold water, so she just stood there sipping the cola a little bit. After all, she was not exerting herself the way Art was, who was now attacking the nuts with vigor and one by one they were coming off. Jacking the car a little higher up, Art extracted the flat tire and quickly put the new one in its place. Screwing the nuts back on proved to be much easier to do than the reverse. Standing up, and putting the tools back in the trunk with the flat tire, Art dusted himself off, polished off the rest of the cola, and then said, "Well, not too bad. We didn't lose more than an hour. Let's head to Urfa and have a nice dinner and process what we saw at Göbeckli Tepe."

The drive was quiet, and Art was still sweating from the exertion. About fifteen minutes down the road, his stomach began to revolt. All of a sudden he jerked the car to the side of the road, threw open the door, and vomited—over and over and over again. "There was something wrong with that drink!" cried Art now shaking all over. "Something not right! Are you okay?"

Marissa noticed her stomach was a little on the rocks as well, but she had swallowed only a few sips. "My stomach aches a little, so let me drive when we are ready to leave. Do you really think that nice little man meant to do us harm?"

"There was something strange. He had already opened the drinks. Why would he do that?" asked Art as he doubled over with cramps once again.

Marissa admitted, "I hardly paid attention to that. You know, he looked a little like the man who took our picture up on Mt. Nemrut. But that man had a big mustache!"

Art's eyebrows raised in recognition. "He did look like the photo guy! Honestly I was so busy just staring at you, that I hardly paid attention to our camera guy. But you realize what this means? If it's the same guy, maybe he's been following us. And if it's the same guy, he shaved off his mustache since yesterday. Why would he do that if not to throw us off? Not good." Art was beginning to feel a bit better having completely emptied the contents of his stomach.

Aziz had experimented with a different poison—arsenic. He wanted the pair to die slowly—in agony—not suddenly like the priest. Apparently, the dosage of arsenic in a can of carbonated soda was enough to make them sick but not enough to kill them.

"I guess we will not be up for dancing the wild fandango tonight in Urfa?" said Marissa trying to defuse the tension.

"I guess not," agreed Art. "But we can snuggle in tonight, and be thankful for a close call. And now we know to be on our guard. Man, what was in that soda?"

With Marissa at the wheel, they breezed by a gas station on the road into Urfa. Standing under the canopy, filling his tank, was Aziz. When he saw the Wests drive by, he yelled an oath in Turkish. Apparently it would take more than arsenic in cola to do away with his third and fourth victims.

26

HOMEWARD BOUND

FOR JOYCE, THE JOURNEY back to North Carolina provided quiet time to mull over her own future. In truth, she needed to sell her house in Charlotte because she wanted to move back to her home town of Wilmington where she already had a condo. Fortunately, all this coincided with Laura's furlough and both knew they were in for a lot of work cleaning up the Charlotte house, organizing a yard sale, and moving what was left to Wilmington.

Jake was rather glum about all this, feeling like he was being kicked out into the real world. He could either find an apartment in Charlotte downtown near the Hornet's arena, or buy his own house or, better yet, get married real soon! He snuck a glance at Melody who seemed to be sleeping. Was she ready to get married? He enjoyed being the gentleman renter in Joyce's house; she was indeed his second mother. He had to admit that he was glad that life in Palestine was now behind him. With his own mother now safely living and working in the monastery near Jericho, all seemed quiet on that home front.

Passport control in Atlanta can take a while. A burly, dark-headed man said in a monotone, "Passport and documents please." Jake traveled with his Jordanian passport. The man looked up twice at Jake as he was scanning the passport and his customs form and then finally pushed a little red button and said, "You'll need to come with me sir."

Jake groaned and replied a bit too testily, "Just great!"

The little sanitized room with benches and high fluorescent lights seemed like the antechamber to an operating room, and Jake found himself blinking profusely in the glare. A very large man eating a doughnut appeared and sat down across from Jake. "So, you've been to Istanbul?"

"Yes sir. I went to a wedding of a family friend," replied Jake glumly.

"And I see you are holding a Jordanian passport, but the information in the passport suggests you are not from Jordan, but rather from Israel?"

"That's right. Before the seven days war, all Palestinians were considered citizens of Jordan and had Jordanian passports because Jordan claimed everything on the West Bank up through east Jerusalem, hence the Jordanian passport."

"But you are a young man. Were you even alive in 1967 or during the Yom Kippur war?"

"No sir, but my mother was, and this passport reflects her citizenship. It's actually a passport for a teenager who travels with a parent."

"But you're not a teenager any more son. And why exactly are you in the United States? And while I am at it, the name Arafat and the town of Bethlehem ring a bell. You wouldn't happen to be a relative of the famous Yassir Arafat?"

Now Jake was really sweating but he tried to remain calm. "It's a common last name. I was brought to the United States by Michael Jordan to play basketball for the Charlotte Hornets. If you call this number, someone there can verify my story." Jake handed over his Hornets ID card. "They took care of my entry into the country, and this is the first time I've travelled overseas on my own. Well, actually, I'm travelling with friends who can also verify my identity—especially my fiancée, Melody! We're all coming back from the same wedding. Look, man, I'm in the process of applying for citizenship, but these things take time."

"They do indeed," said the man as he munched on his doughnut. Just then another TSA agent came in and his face suddenly lit up. "Hey, you look mighty familiar. Aren't you the guy with the Hornets who lit up the Atlanta Hawks in April for 34 or so points including several monster dunks like those of Blake Griffin?"

Jake finally smiled and said, "Yep, that would be me!"

"You recognize this guy?' said the doughnut eater.

"Sure, he's Jake the Cat Arafat, a slick hoopster. Take Mr. Arafat and get his passport stamped and let him through!"

Turning to Jake he said, "Sorry for the hassle but we can't be too careful these days, especially since bin Laden was killed."

"I understand," said Jake as he shook the hand of both TSA agents—and gave them his autograph on an airport notepad!

Melody was especially nervous as they waited for Jake. Actually, Laura hadn't fared much better. Three agents poured over her complicated passport that was now filled with stamps entering and leaving all sort of Asian countries!

"Your TSA boys are thorough. But it's a good thing somebody recognized me. I might have been in there for hours. And before you ask, no, I did not tell them I'm a relative of Yassir Arafat!"

"A darn good thing, or I might have been bailing you out of jail," said Joyce. "Now we need to scoot to catch the commuter flight back to Charlotte. Home, sweet home is calling, and I can't wait to get to that four poster bed. I like everything about traveling except the traveling part!"

"Amen to that," said L.J.

～

The following morning, she checked the time difference and concluded, "Now is the right time for me to ring Arthur." After four rings, finally her son picked up, and she could hear coughing on the other end of the line. "You're not catching a cold are you?"

"No Mom, nothing like that." He couldn't imagine filling her in with the day's events. So he bypassed all that and said, "So, what's up?"

"What's up is the Patriarch in Istanbul wants to talk with you, and I totally forgot to tell you this on the wedding day. We were more than a little preoccupied with other matters, and it slipped my mind."

"No problem, did he say what he wants?"

"On the one hand, he implied it was important. On the other hand, he implied it could wait until after the wedding at least or even the honeymoon. But I still think you should give him a ring if you can. By the way, where are you?"

"I'm in the wilds of Eastern Turkey! Where are you?"

"I'm in my Charlotte kitchen having a morning coffee! We all got in last night."

"That's good to know. I'm glad you're all safe. I'm guessing L.J. is finding home a little strange after all these years in New Guinea. Take her to some of the new restaurants around!"

"We're all going out tonight. And then Jake and Melody will probably go back to Wilmington for awhile. Now it's time for their wedding plans to begin."

"I'm glad you all made it to our wedding—as unconventional as it was!"

"What are you talking about—wild horses couldn't have kept me away! Love you, bye."

The phone went silent, and Art flipped it closed, lost in thought.

"So what was that all about?" asked Marissa quietly.

"Oh probably nothing important. My mother just told me the Turkish equivalent of the Pope needs to talk with me sooner rather than later," said Art trying to suppress a laugh.

"Art West, are you serious! You're wanted by the Patriarch?"

"Apparently so."

"Can this honeymoon get any stranger?"

"I'd rather not think of the ways it could get stranger. I will call the Patriarch tomorrow morning. For now, I just want to settle in for the night, because that little man was more than a little unsettling. In fact you could say he turned my stomach!"

"That's fine, tonight we have other fish to fry."

"Or grits to boil."

"Or müjver to consume."

"Now you're talking! Okay so who just won the pun contest?"

Marissa just sighed and said, "I can see you've already had too much of an intoxicating effect on me. I'm even talking like you, bad jokes and all."

"You know the old joke about marriage," said Art with a grin.

Marissa just raised her eyebrows and shook her head.

"The only question that remains after the two become one is—which one???"

27

MANUSCRIPTS ROCKEFELLER

THE ROCKEFELLER MUSEUM, FORMERLY the Palestine Archaeological Museum, sits atop a little hill on the border between the old city and the new Israeli city of Jerusalem. It now houses a nice collection of artifacts plus the main office of the Israeli Antiquities Authority (IAA). To some extent it has become a processing center for recent finds. Director Sammy Cohen was sitting at his cluttered desk muttering to himself about the increasing amount of paperwork he was expected to do to satisfy the Israeli government that all was well with the IAA.

Sammy, who had lost the sweepstakes for Grace's heart to computer mogul Manny Cohen, nonetheless continued to carry some affection for Grace, and admiration for her knowledge and integrity as a scholar. She was now late for their meeting, and he was beginning to fidget. What he needed right now was an excuse to ignore the mountain of paperwork on his desk. Just then he heard a car come screeching to a halt at the top of the circular drive, and a loud voice telling the new security guard, "Look, you should know better than to stop me for questioning. I'm Dr. Grace Levine, and I have an important meeting with Director Cohen. If you need to move my little Mazda Miata, here are the keys!"

Sammy ran to the entrance way of the museum to rescue the new security guard, but Grace ran up the stairs and gave Sammy a hug saying, "Forget about it Sam. We have far more important things to attend to now."

"Right you are," said Sammy beaming after her warm embrace and greeting. "Let's take a right turn here and head down to the inspection room where the manuscript is housed."

The inspection room, as Sammy called it, was little more than a windowless, high-ceilinged, thick-walled chamber retro-fitted with access pads, locked cabinets, bullet-proof glass cases, microscopes and the like. Yet lying on the main table unrolled and under glass was a manuscript—hopefully a first century manuscript.

"I've talked to Rami, so I have my questions about provenance answered. So now it's just me and the letters on those pages!"

Sammy said, "Grace, I will just leave you locked in here for a while. Use the recorder for all your initial thoughts. There's an intercom over there on the wall where you can call me in my office when you are ready to tell me something. The room is yours!"

"Will do," said Grace, adjusting her small red glasses and beginning to pour over the manuscript. "One question—is this all of it?"

"Yes, all we found was a manuscript with about 500 lines total, and it does appear to be the whole manuscript, but I will let you weigh in on that," said Sammy as he walked to the door and quietly closed it behind him.

Grace, like Art, was a person capable of tunnel vision when she was concentrating on something as fascinating as an ancient manuscript. She lost all track of time and place when she started reading the text with a magnifying glass. Turning on the recorder she began to cover the basics emphatically.

"Clearly this is Aramaic writing but not as late as the Amoraic period, so not mid-third century. So, this is either a first or second century Aramaic manuscript. I'm seeing a fair and steady hand from a scribe who knew exactly how to line out a papyrus and use all of its space efficiently. I think he used the usual black soot sort of ink and a stylus. The letters are carefully formed, and we have here *scriptio continua*, a continuous flow of letters, except there seem to be five or six small breaks. Could these be subsections? The papyrus itself is of good quality, though frayed at the edges."

After the initial physical analysis, Grace started to read little bits of the manuscript—translating into the recorder. Yes, these were sayings of Jesus. No, an initial scan of the 500 lines did not suggest any new ones, but she would need to go over it inch by inch before anything definitive could be concluded. And when she got to the Beatitudes it became clear that this manuscript was definitely following one particular strain of Q material—the Matthean one.

Recorder on, she stated, "Note the use of the 'poor in spirit' phrase. Also note the writer uses 'debts' rather than 'trespasses' in the Lord's prayer." Two hours had passed, and Grace realized she needed to wrap up her initial investigation.

Getting up from the table and pushing the intercom button she said, "Sammy, time to let the bird out of the cage. I have some tentative news for you. Also, can you provide a photocopy of the whole thing?"

When Sammy entered the room, he handed her the photocopy and asked, "What do you think?"

Grace was quick to reply. "No question it's early Aramaic from the first or second century, and equally no question it's the sayings of Jesus. I saw precious little evidence of narrative, so I think this must be some sort of collection of early sayings, whether we call it Q or not. And what this means is that the sayings of Jesus must have been written down before the production of Matthew's and Luke's Gospels, something most scholars already thought likely, but now they will be happy to have some confirmation of that theory. Also, I see no sign of any of the Gospel of Thomas's eccentric or unique sayings either. I always thought that was an odd second century collection anyway. You can listen to all my ramblings on the tape later!"

"I'll probably enjoy that," said Sammy smiling. "It's late but the crew at *Ha'Aretz* never sleeps, and the editor is eager to hear what we have to say. I will accompany you so we can both make pronouncements—the testimony of two witnesses and all that."

"Sounds like a good plan. I'll call Manny and tell him I'll be very late. Unfortunately, he's getting used to that," she added with a sigh. "And, by the way, I'll drive!"

"The last time I was in your little red coupe, I nearly had a heart attack. Let me get my meds before we leave!" insisted Sammy.

Grace just laughed. The new security guard retrieved her pass before she ran out the door. When, not if, she came again, he had no doubt that he would remember her.

28

MARY'S HOUSE REVISITED

IT WAS 9 AM the next morning when Art called the Patriarch at his office. "Your Excellence, this is Art West calling at your request. I am sorry not to get back to you in a more timely manner but, as you know I just got married. Do forgive me for my tardiness."

"Not a problem, my son. I want to discuss a matter that is both biblical and archaeological. But what I have to discuss with you must be said in absolute privacy. Are you alone?"

"No sir. Marissa is here with me, and I might add that she is a recognized archaeologist also. I would like to include her if it's appropriate. Both of us have dealt with highly confidential scholastic matters in the past."

There was a pause at the other end of the line, while the Patriarch mulled over Art's request. "I will agree to this, but I am trying to limit the number of people who know about this matter. It must remain absolutely secret until I can determine what to do about it. Am I being clear?"

"Perfectly clear," promised Art. "I'm listening."

Taking a deep breath, the Patriarch said, "I am going to read to you the English summary made for me by one of our priests, as my English is not perfect. It is rather long, but sets the stage for the new information that has come to light.

The House of the Virgin Mary is a Christian and Muslim shrine located on Mt. Koressos near Ephesus and Selchuk. Pilgrims visit the house based on the belief that Mary, the mother of Jesus, was taken to this stone house by the Beloved Disciple, traditionally assumed to be St. John, and lived there until her bodily Assumption (according to Catholic doctrine) or Dormition (according to Orthodox belief). In other words, Catholics, Orthodox and Muslims all have a vested interest in the authenticity and sacredness of this site.

At the beginning of the 19th century, Anne Catherine Emmerich (1774–1824), a bedridden Augustinian nun in Germany, reported a series of visions in which she recounted the last days of the life of Jesus and details of the life of Mary. Emmerich was known in Germany as a mystic and was visited by a number of notable figures.

One of Emmerich's visitors was Clemens Brentano (1778–1842) who after a first visit, stayed in Dülmen for five years (1818–1824) to transcribe her visions. After Emmerich's death, Brentano published a book based on his transcriptions of her reported visions, and a second book was published based on his notes after his own death. It should be strongly noted that the Vatican does not endorse the authenticity of these books, and many believe that his writings are either fabrications or fictitious elaborations of the actual words of Emmerich.

One of Emmerich's accounts was a description of a house the Beloved Disciple built in Ephesus for Mary where she had lived to the end of her life. Emmerich provided a number of details about the location of the house, and the topography of the surrounding area.

Emmerich claimed the house was built with rectangular stones, that the windows were high up near the flat roof and that it consisted of two parts with a hearth at the center of the house. She further described the location of the doors, the shape of the chimney, etc. The book containing these descriptions was published in 1852 in Munich.

On October 18, 1881, relying on the descriptions in the book by Brentano based on his conversations with Emmerich, a French priest, the Abbé Julien Gouyet, discovered a small stone building on a mountain overlooking the ruins of ancient Ephesus in Turkey. He believed it was the house described by Emmerich and where the Virgin Mary had lived the final years of her life. Abbé Gouyet's discovery was not taken seriously, but ten years later, urged by Sister Marie de Mandat-Grancey, two priests rediscovered the building in 1891, using the same source for a guide.

Apparently, the four-walled, roofless ruin had been venerated for a long time by the members of a distant mountain village who were descended from the Christians of Ephesus. In Turkish, the house is called *Panaya*

Kapulu ("Doorway to the Virgin"). Every year pilgrims go to the site on August 15, the date on which most of the Christian world celebrates Mary's Dormition/Assumption.

Sister Marie de Mandat-Grancey was named Foundress of Mary's House by the Catholic Church and was responsible for acquiring, restoring and preserving the building and surrounding areas of the mountain from 1891 until her death in 1915. The discovery revived and strengthened a Christian tradition dating from the 12th century, the tradition of Ephesus, which has competed with the older Jerusalem tradition about the place of the Blessed Virgin's Dormition. Due to the actions of Pope Leo XIII in 1896 and Pope John XXIII in 1961, the Catholic Church first removed plenary indulgences from the Church of the Dormition in Jerusalem and then bestowed them to pilgrims to Mary's House in Ephesus.

The restored portion of the structure has been distinguished from the original remains of the structure by a line painted in red. Some have expressed doubt about the site, as the tradition of Mary's association with Ephesus arose only in the twelfth century, while the universal tradition among the Fathers of the Church places her residence in Jerusalem. Supporters of the Ephesus tradition base their belief on the presence in Ephesus of the 5th century Church of Mary, the first basilica in the world dedicated to the Virgin Mary.

The Roman Catholic Church has never pronounced on the authenticity of the house, for lack of scientifically acceptable evidence. It has, however, from the blessing of the first pilgrimage by Pope Leo XIII in 1896, taken a positive attitude towards the site. Pope Pius XII, in 1951, following the definition of the dogma of the Assumption in 1950, elevated the house to the status of a Holy Place, a privilege later made permanent by Pope John XXIII. The site is venerated by Muslims as well as Christians. Pilgrims drink from a spring under the house which is believed to have healing properties. A liturgical ceremony is held here every year on August 15 to commemorate the Assumption of Mary.

Pope Paul VI visited the shrine in 1967, and "unofficial-ly" confirmed its authenticity. Pope John Paul II also visited the shrine in 1979 followed by Pope Benedict in 2006 during his four-day pastoral trip to Turkey.[1]

The Patriarch finished reading, took a breath, and said, "Have you any questions thus far? I am sure you can see what an important site this is for many Christians and Muslims."

"That is clear to me, and thank you for refreshing my memory on some of the traditions and introducing me to others I was not aware of. I was especially unaware of the connection with Anne Catherine Emmerich, whose 'Dolorous Passion of the Christ' provided the colorful material for much of Mel Gibson's movie, The Passion of the Christ. That is intriguing. But I'm sure you didn't want me to call you so you could better inform me about things that are already common knowledge. What is troubling you, if I may ask?"

"What is troubling me is what has been found in the crypt beneath this house. A skeleton of a small woman was found there, carefully buried. DNA and other sorts of testing show that this woman was from the Ancient Near East, possibly dating to the first century A.D. Furthermore, around her neck was a golden amulet or locket of sorts with a picture of a woman embracing a cross on it, and were that not enough, inside the locket was a small piece of papyrus identifying the woman as Mary—in Aramaic."

There was such a long silent pause at the other end of the line while this was sinking in that finally Bartholomew said, "Are you still there Professor?"

"Yes, yes I am! This is stunning news! In one sense it is good news, as the site will become even more of a pilgrimage place and you have positive confirmation that someone named Mary was actually there. But there's the bad news! If, and I say if, the body is that of Mary, the Mother of Jesus, its

1. Some of this information is from the Wikipedia article on the House of Mary in Ephesus accessed January 3, 2012 (http://en.wikipedia.org/wiki/House_of_the_Virgin_Mary).

existence refutes traditional Catholic, Orthodox, and even Muslim traditions about the bodily Assumption of Mary.

There was a sigh at the other end of the line, and finally Bartholomew
said, "You are well informed. We would not be celebrating a Feast of the
Assumption if we had made a false assumption about that."

After another pause for reflection Art asked, "How can I help you in this
matter? As a Protestant, I don't believe in the historical assumption of Mary
into heaven. I believe that faith should not go against the historical evidence."

"After much prayer, this is precisely why I would like you to come and
have a look at the archaeological evidence and either confirm it, or make
clear to me that the evidence is not quite certain or clear. Since you do not
have a vested interest in this doctrine, no one could accuse you of slanting
the evidence in favor of such a doctrine. Will you do it?"

"I would be honored—as soon as my honeymoon is over."

"Of course, of course! Shall we talk again soon?"

Sitting upright on the bed, Art said, "I will call you the beginning of
next week, and we will set up a time for us to examine the evidence."

After the usual goodbyes, Art turned to Marissa who had a quizzical
look on her face and blurted out, "It appears they may have found Mary or
at least a Mary!"

"Which Mary? Not the mother of Jesus Mary!"

"That's the big question. They found a Mary buried under the so-called
House of Mary near Ephesus. As you know, according to some, Mary the
mother of Jesus ascended bodily into heaven—from Ephesus or Jerusalem
depending upon the tradition."

"And you are saying they have proof positive that the skeleton is hers?"

"I don't know about proof, but it sounds like they have some evidence.
Do you have any idea what a bombshell this will be if it becomes public
knowledge? And it's not just Christians who will be shocked—don't forget
the Muslims. I told the Patriarch that we could look into it for him," said Art
with a hopeful tone of voice.

"Well, yes, but next time, ask me first," said Marissa pursing her lips.

"Right! This newly married thing is a work in progress. And speaking
of our honeymoon, while I love a good archaeological site, let's finish it out
with less touring and more pampering. We really need some down time!"

"I couldn't agree more," said Marissa laughing. "Let's get out of here!"

29

ABDULLAH'S ALIAS

ABDULLAH HASHIMI WAS NOT your average Palestinian. For one thing, he was rather light skinned, like other Palestinians with Jordanian roots. For another, he had shaved off all his hair, so he rather resembled a bald eagle with a prominent Middle Eastern beak. But perhaps most surprisingly, he changed his name legally to Saul Levi after at least outwardly converting to Judaism. It was his rabbi who recommended him to Sammy Cohen as a good prospect for their new front door security guard. The rabbi had watched Saul do all kinds of *mitzwoth* (good deeds) for the synagogue, and since he said he had been in the security business for some time, he seemed a logical candidate, not least because he was 6'3" and weighed 240. He looked like a middle linebacker, but he was as soft spoken as a librarian.

It was a good cover. What no one knew, not even Sammy after the basic background checks, was that Abdullah was a stealth agent of Hamas, and his mission was to fill up their coffers by stealing and selling antiquities. The reason the background check had produced nothing of note is because Saul Levi was a real person who looked rather like Abdullah, but *that* Saul Levi had gone on a Mediterranean cruise and never came home. He was murdered at sea by Hamas and his place immediately taken by Abdullah in as slick a case of stolen identity as one could imagine.

Abdullah was very excited. After working for three months at the Rockefeller quietly establishing rapport with the staff of the IAA, on this morning he was going to be left all alone on the premises, with the building closed to the public. It was Shabbat. And he had access to the scriptorium.

At the end of the day he began his rounds of the building, and the security cameras watched his progress. He entered each room, checked them out and then left. But when he entered the documents room, he covered the camera lens temporarily and quickly removed the manuscript.

Abdullah planned to let Sammy discover the theft when he returned to work on Monday. And then, if things got too hot in a week or so, Abdullah would go to Sammy and tell him he felt like he had failed in properly guarding the property, and he would quietly resign. Perfect! Of course no human plan is ever perfect. While the day had gone by quietly without incident, what Abdullah had not counted on was Sammy forgetting his glasses at the office, and returning at sundown to retrieve them—right when Abdullah was preparing to leave the building with the manuscript hidden in the lining of his jacket.

"Saul, glad I caught you," said Sammy as he ran up the stairs. "Hold the door for a minute. I've got to go to the office and get my glasses which I left yesterday in my haste to get to synagogue."

Abdullah dutifully held the door and waited, sweat beginning to trickle down his back. It seemed like an eternity before Sammy returned after rummaging through piles of papers to find his glasses. As he came back out the door, he said, "Thanks so much for looking after things so well. We've been very proud of your work thus far. Very careful and thorough." And with this he patted Saul on the back and ran down the stairs to his waiting car.

The guard called out, "Thank you, sir!"

Abdullah locked the door, waved to Sammy, and exhaled loudly. And then he drove off to meet an antiquities dealer in the Jewish quarter.

30

BEACH LIFE

GULLS WERE CIRCLING OVERHEAD looking for yet another fishing boat to raid, and making a racket which woke Art West. There curled up on his shoulder was his beautiful bronze wife. Art lay there quietly gazing at her, and saying a silent prayer of thanks for this great new blessing in his life. Yes, he knew it meant lots of mid-life adjustments, but he was at peace with that.

Quietly he slipped out of the bed, threw on his shorts, and opened the glass door that led to the little balcony in the honeymoon suite. Last night had been all joy and ecstasy. Art was telling himself he could get used to this. He had never felt so close to another human being, not even his parents or sister. He wondered if along side the category 'mid-life crisis' there was another one called 'mid-life blessing'? "God is good all the time," he whispered to himself.

Their flight from far-eastern Turkey brought them to sunny Konyaalti Beach near Antalya which came highly recommended by the Cohens. Nothing at all was planned for this day, except for beach combing, swimming, and lots of good seafood. Art figured he could suffer through that quite nicely. And if Marissa wanted some excitement at the water park, then he could do that too!

Marissa soon joined him on the balcony. "Let's go to Kismet Balikcisi for lunch." My friends tell me it's the best fish in town. You can pick out the fish you want. Then they weigh it and prepare it. Can you imagine!"

"I love seafood—if I see food I eat it!" promised Art. "Meltem said that we need to make our last meal here special; in short, we are going to the Balik Evi on Lara Road which overlooks the beautiful Mediterranean of course. Whatever's in that water, it will be on the menu! Would you recommend I try the octopus?"

"As part of the *meze*, yes. After that, more fresh fish!"

They collectively sighed just thinking about meals to come before they had too many things to do.

Just then Art's cellphone went off, playing the Beatles "All You Need Is Love."

"Hello," said Art rather cautiously thinking he should have just shut it off.

"Grace here, and you better be sitting down my friend."

"Well, I'm sitting on a balcony in Antalya overlooking the water—it's as pretty as you promised. So nice to hear from you—what's up?"

"What's up is something potentially bigger than your Papias scrolls and the James ossuary put together."

"Okay, you've peaked my interest! What is it?"

"It looks like they have found Q in Capernaum, and it's in Aramaic no less!"

"You're pulling my leg, right?"

"Nope, I don't make long distance calls to pull your leg on your honeymoon."

"So how do you know it is what you think it is?"

"I've done some preliminary studies but things are looking good. You sure you don't want to take a little detour to Jerusalem from Antalya? I'd like to be able to tell the authorities that you and Marissa might be available."

"I'll have to talk with the boss about that. But call me back later when you're more sure of things."

"Will do, *mazel tov*!" And with that Grace rang off.

"Grace says they've found Jesus' Greatest Hits in Aramaic no less!"

Marissa just giggled and said, "I knew marrying you was not going to be boring."

～

The Cohens always spent their weekends at their beach front house in Tel Aviv. Grace often retreated to her study on the second floor overlooking the ocean. The breezes tempered the blazing sun. Grace was content to stay at home, pour over her photocopy of the Q document, and spend some quality time with Yelena. With a small book easel on which she propped up the scroll photocopy and her MacBook Pro humming she was carefully translating the document line by line and pondering the meaning. There could be no doubt that this was a landmark discovery which could change the face of NT studies. As she sipped her coffee, she smiled and said to herself, "For sure, some literate person in Capernaum made a collection of Jesus' famous sayings, and not just in any form, but in a more Matthean form."

Grace still had three columns to translate, but the form of the Lord's prayer had been especially interesting. For one thing it did not have the doxology, which most scholars already thought was added later. But, the Aramaic made clearer the reading of the last two lines, "Put us not to the test, and deliver us from the Evil One." And yes, the Aramaic form had "give us today the bread for tomorrow."

"This makes sense as a prayer of a rather poor person who lives day by day, and hand to mouth," mused Grace.

Suddenly, Manny bounced into the room saying, "Can I distract you long enough to take you to lunch at our favorite little crab shack down the road? I'm starving!"

"How can I refuse? Despite my Jewish reservations, crustaceans and I go way back and are very fond of each other. I've even eaten yabbies and bugs in Cairns, Down Under."

"Bugs? Have you gone all John the Baptist on me?"

"No dear, those are the colloquial names for crayfish and lobster-like creatures that you eat in Australia. Call Yelena. She's in her room, and wants to go to a local bookshop, which we can do right after lunch."

Here was a couple who loved the security of having someone in their lives to share even the simplest of moments. Even better, they loved being new parents with a bright, newly-turned teenage daughter. Yahweh had truly blessed them.

31

THAT OLD BLACK MARKET MAGIC

THE UNDERBELLY OF THE antiquities trade in Jerusalem was the black market, which despite the best efforts of the IAA and the antiquities police continued to thrive in Jerusalem. Abdullah had been wise enough to set up the deal for the manuscript well in advance of the heist, so that the exchange could be made quickly. He would be dealing with a one-eyed man known as Omar, and no one seemed to know his full name. He operated out of the back of a deli not far from Kahlil and Hannah's antiquities shop. The man was strictly low profile, and he only came out of hiding when a deal was going down. Omar was alleged to have Iranian contacts who bankrolled his activities for a profit. And he dealt strictly in cash—preferably euros or US dollars.

The Mehane Yehuda Market was quiet on the sabbath—only a few restaurants remained open. The hundreds of vendors were home with their families. The Israeli guards who usually stood watch had also gone home for the evening. There was very little foot traffic through the *shuk* [marketplace], as the locals called it.

Abdullah hurried down the alleys until he reached a shop called Mohammed's Café. Looking both ways to make very sure he was not being followed, he walked into a dimly lit room where there was only one elderly man drinking java at a corner table, and a man behind the deli case. Abdullah went up to the counter and asked, "Omar?" The swarthy attendant simply pointed his thumb to the curtain which separated the front from the back of the shop.

Abdullah found himself in a room smelling of fried food from the adjacent kitchen. Omar looked up from his Arabic newspaper and said, "So do you have it?"

"Of course. I would not have come if I didn't. But the better question is, do you have the money?"

"No one need question Omar about money. I have it here under my chair in the safety deposit bag," explained Omar matter-of-factly.

"So let's take care of business. We agreed on $3 million USD right?"

"Right, less my commission which is $25,000, since I am taking the risk of handling a hot item and you will be free and clear shortly."

Abdullah groaned but nodded yes, and the exchange was made quickly.

"If I were you, I would go out the back and leave the *shuk* by way of the Holy Sepulchre and the gate nearest it. Then you can double back to your car."

Abdullah simply added, "*Shukran* [thank you], and *Allahu Akbar* [God is great]."

"*Allahu Akbar*," replied Omar, and he too slipped out the back and into the darkening corridors of the market.

～

Sunday came and went quietly enough, but on Monday, Sammy had occasion to go to the documents room. And while his purpose in going was not to ogle the Q document again, nevertheless he took a look in the glass case, and nearly passed out. Bracing himself on the case itself he started yelling down the hall to his secretary Myra.

"Get the security guard quick!"

In minutes Saul came running down the hall, breathless, yelling, "What's wrong?"

"What's wrong is that we've had a break in and the priceless Aramaic Q document is missing! Who could do this and who would? We'd best call the police immediately. This is now a crime scene!"

"Yes sir. I'm terribly sorry about this. It must have happened in the middle of the night. This must have been a very professional thief!"

"Very! Come with me!" barked Sammy, running his hand through what was left of his hair. Back in his office, Sammy went into the adjoining room where the security systems were kept. Going back to Saturday, he ran through the tape and discovered a blank period of at least thirty seconds around the same time that he himself had been in the building fetching his glasses! "The police will have to see this—thirty seconds is plenty of time to remove the manuscript. As I remember, we both left the building together."

"Yes sir! I am terribly sorry about this! If this breach of security is going to compromise my good name or standing here, I would prefer to just resign quietly."

"Nonsense," said Sammy. "You came highly recommended, and you've done a good job. I doubt that a thief of this caliber would have problems with one guard. If you had been there—you would probably be dead!"

32

PARIS CALLING

OMAR WAS NO ORDINARY Palestinian black market dealer, despite his gruff, back-alley appearance. Omar was a person with contacts all over the world for whatever needed to be done. Sunday he supervised the preparation of phony supporting documents. Monday morning saw him walking through Charles De Gaulle Airport heading for the taxi stand. He had an important meeting in downtown Paris with Henri L'Matin who often served as a broker for antiquities to the Louvre.

It was a bright but humid day and Omar was glad he brought his sunglasses. Sporting a new suit, a small roller suitcase, and a leather document tube, he had come to consummate a transaction and leave town as quickly as possible. The taxi wound through the busy streets and eventually came to an office complex near St. Chapelle. It was a pity he didn't have time to do a little sightseeing and sample the wonderful cuisine, but such was his life. Someday, perhaps after this sale, he could retire and do such things.

Henri L'Matin was no ordinary entrepreneur. He was what Americans called a wheeler-dealer, and he drove a hard bargain. Henri brought to the meeting his own expert in ancient Aramaic documents to authenticate what was safely hidden in Omar's document tube.

Walking up the stairs into the office complex, Omar was buzzed in by the security guard, and was met almost immediately by a beautiful secretary wearing a bright green low-cut dress and matching high heels. Ah, Paris fashion, what a change from what conservative women wore in Palestine.

"*Bonjour*, Monsieur Omar. If you will please come with me we will go right through to Monsieur L'Matin's office. He is waiting for you. I trust your trip was uneventful?" said Claire.

"*Très bon*," said Omar in his rusty French. Only the real moguls of French industry had offices this elegant. The huge polished mahogany door was opened by the secretary and Omar was ushered in without fanfare.

"Monsieur Omar, it is a pleasure to see you once again. I gather you have something rather special for me this time?" said the man in the three-piece suit with the carefully quaffed hairdo.

"Indeed, I do. The rarest of rarities. For you I have a first century A.D. manuscript that not merely mentions Jesus but is a compendium of his sayings in his own language—Aramaic. There is nothing like this anywhere else in the world. It could be called the Gospel of Jesus. My contacts have authenticated this document. And I have proper documents for you. I can tell you that it was found on an archaeological dig in Capernaum in the 1960s."

With a flourish, Omar put on his gloves, carefully opened the document tube, and ever so gently extracted the scroll. Space had been cleared on the expansive glass top desk of the entrepreneur so they could look at the document itself. Over L'Matin's shoulder one could see Notre Dame through the vast expanse of glass. Five minutes turned into ten minutes turned into twenty minutes as both L'Matin and his manuscript expert, Prof. Garrard Dupuis, continued their examination.

Omar coughed and said, "I believe you can see the remarkable quality and, I might add, condition of this manuscript. So, shall we get down to business?"

"Yes, but let me first ask the opinion of Prof. Garrard."

"This appears to be a genuine document of such great importance that I would advise you Monsieur L'Matin not to miss this opportunity to purchase it," stated the professor emphatically.

L'Matin cleared his throat and said, "Would $20 million U.S. be sufficient?"

Omar smiled. "Yes. It can be wired to my Swiss Bank account at Banque d'Swisse in Geneva."

"I am buzzing my secretary now."

Claire came through the door almost immediately. Omar was led to her computer where he keyed in the confidential numbers. She finished the simple transaction and escorted him back to the inner office. "I will print a copy of the paperwork for you," she promised.

For the next five minutes Monsieur L'Matin pumped Omar for any sort of information he could give about the document. Omar was happy to talk about its background, or provenance as the scholars put it, but not about how he obtained the document. On that point he said, "I can assure you that I bought the document. You have the papers. I trust this sale will remain confidential like the previous ones and you will not reveal my identity to anyone."

"*Bien sur*," replied L'Matin with a smile. "I am the soul of discretion in such matters."

Omar handed the document case over to L'Matin, turned on his smartphone, brought up the application that connected him to his bank account, saw that the money had been deposited, smiled, closed his phone, and then rose to leave. After shaking hands, he followed Claire down the hall to the front entrance, and out onto the streets of Paris. "I shall celebrate tonight, and head home tomorrow morning. The Champs Elysee is calling me," said an ebullient antiquities dealer who had just pulled off the deal of his life. A little thought crept into his head. "Perhaps it might be wise for me to disappear for a while. And where better to disappear than in beautiful France."

33

GRACE NOTES

THERE ARE PHONE CALLS that one never wants to get, and this morning's phone call made Grace Levine spitting mad. Sammy called to tell her that the Q document had been stolen, whereabouts unknown.

Grace was just thankful that photocopies had been made in advance. But there were things about this theft that were peculiar. Was the thief already in the building when the doors were locked for the night? How did the thief get the access codes? Obviously, the thief covered up the camera while he stole the manuscript. He or she knew the layout of the building and the scriptorium. In the back of her mind, she was sure this was either an inside job or the thief had help on the inside. The antiquities police would have to explore all the options.

Meanwhile, after making the translation of the Q scroll, Grace proceeded to examine the text in more detail. First, she outlined the physical properties of the scroll and the language used. Secondly, she discussed how the document was composed, especially noting the little divisions that occurred five or six times in the scroll. Thirdly, she noted the lack of narrative, with rare exception. For example, there was the telling of the baptism and temptation of Jesus at the beginning of the scroll. But why leave out so much narrative and include so many sayings with very little narrative context?

Moving on she outlined her fourth point. What should be made of the almost uniformly Matthean form of the sayings? Was this really the earliest form of the Jesus tradition, or was this a re-Judaizing of the tradition, for example, changing Kingdom of God into Kingdom of Heaven?

After mulling a bit she penned a fifth note. Was this document intended to be a sort of Pentateuch-like collection of Jesus' teaching? Following the Pentateuch, the Q document could be the "five books of Jesus." But that didn't explain the apparent six breaks in the manuscript. And Grace noticed that the major theme and presentation linking the subsections was revealing Jesus to be a messianic sage, not a prophet and not really all that much like Moses. The presentation seemed to focus more on Jesus as a figure like unto but greater than Solomon. Why?

And then there was point number six. Who is going to use this document? Was it meant to be used by converted Jews to defend their faith in Jesus, in short, to do apologetics? Was this part of the interaction between Pharisees and the followers of Jesus in Capernaum? If only the document could be dated more precisely, but Grace could think of no reason it couldn't have come from the first century A.D. and maybe even before the fall of the Temple in A.D. 70.

After staring at her list and munching on two bunches of red grapes, she finally ended with point seven. What was clear to Grace was that this document was not intended to be a Gospel, if by Gospel one meant the story of Jesus from womb to tomb. No, this was some sort of teaching or pedagogical document not focused on story-telling about Jesus, but at the same time, not avoiding all story-telling either. The similarities with the Gospel of Thomas should be reflected on more carefully, she thought.

Grace continued to ponder these matters and hope that she didn't miss anything really important. She got dressed in a nice black and white business suit with black high heels, and prepared to head off to Jerusalem to help Sammy and others with the aftermath of the theft.

Yelena was at the beach for the day with a new friend who recently moved in next door. Manny had things well in hand with his computer business, so he spent the day at the basketball arena in Tel Aviv with his team, Maccabee Elite. After all, he owned the business and the team and could set his own schedule for both! He was wise enough to give Grace a wide berth after that distressing phone call from Sammy.

It was already a hot ninety degree day in Tel Aviv when Grace backed out her red Mazda, revved up the engine, and prepared to scoot down the new four-lane highway to Jerusalem. One thing for sure, it was not going to be a boring day.

34

THE LOUVRE MANEUVER

MONSIEUR HENRI L'MATIN WAS looking supremely confident in his pale blue suit and polished black dress shoes. He was accompanied by his regular bodyguard Hans, a behemoth of 6'8" and 280 pounds, who doubled as his chauffeur. Today, with any luck he would come home with a cool $40 million USD from the sale of this incredible manuscript. Pierre Saint-Saens would be meeting L'Matin at the back door of the Louvre and they would proceed to the acquisitions room in the basement of the famous museum.

L'Matin had no concerns about anything going wrong with the transaction, so eager to see and acquire this manuscript had Saint-Saens sounded on the phone. Indeed, Saint-Saens had arranged a small press conference in the recital hall in the Louvre for an important announcement later that day. The head religion editor of *Le Monde* had been especially alerted that something big was in the works. The Louvre naturally had benefitted from all kinds of extra tourist business and attention in the wake of the *Da Vinci Code,* but this was even bigger than that phony novel. Saint-Saens envisioned making up the cost of the document within a very few years, through premium ticket sales to the special "Gospel of Jesus" exhibit that would be on permanent display in the Louvre. What a coup! And wouldn't the other great European museums like the ones in Berlin and London be jealous! Saint-Saens had visions dancing in his head of the Louvre becoming the world's leading museum once more.

The two security guards at the back door of the Louvre were both armed to the teeth. The Louvre had been the victim of several break-ins in recent years, so extra security had been hired. L'Matin was not personally worried about the matter, since once he turned over the document, it was not his concern.

Saint-Saens met L'Matin at the back door and personally ushered him down a narrow dimly lit corridor into a surprisingly small but well lit and squeaky clean documents room. Lying on the table was already a potential Deed of Title document for the signing. Pointing to three rather comfortable chairs, Saint-Saens, L'Matin and his body guard all sat down, while one of the Louvre guards stood sentinel at the door which was promptly shut and locked. Sitting behind a desk was an elderly scholar, André Proust, waiting his moment to inspect the document.

"First things first," said Saint-Saens. "Tell me how you came to have this precious scroll."

Clearing his throat, L'Matin said, "As you already know, I am a legitimate collector of antiquities. No one has ever accused me of selling artifacts illegally! This scroll was bought from an antiquities dealer in Jerusalem who wishes to remain anonymous. My expert claims this is most definitely a first or second century scroll written in Aramaic. It came from Capernaum, a dig in Galilee. There is no possibility this is some modern forgery; the only question is how ancient is the script."

Taking the scroll case out of his briefcase, L'Matin stood up and handed the scroll to Prof. Proust. "I am sure I don't need to stress that you will please be careful," said L'Matin rather condescendingly.

"*Bien sur,*" said the professor a bit offended. Proust took the scroll case, gently opened it, and even more gently unrolled the scroll, placing tiny brass weights on either end to hold the scroll fully open on the table. There was stony silence in the room as the examination dragged on, and L'Matin could even hear his bodyguard breathing.

Finally, Prof. Proust said, "In view of the known provenance of the scroll, I see no reason at all to doubt this is an early Christian document, very early indeed because it is in Aramaic. Note I did not say Syriac, nor is it in later Amoraic period Aramaic. Furthermore, it is not in Aramaic like that found in Daniel, from before the turn of the Christian era. So yes, clearly enough it is from the first or second century A.D. And there can be no doubt at all that we have here a collection of Jesus' sayings in their Aramaic form, presumably close to their original form, since Jesus spoke

Aramaic. What is most interesting is that on a cursory look it appears to have the form of sayings we generally have in Matthew's Gospel, not Luke's. I say this by examining these third and fourth columns here that contain the Beatitudes and the Lord's Prayer. This finding will confound many Q specialists who want to argue that Luke's version of these sayings is more primitive. These are questions for later scholarly debate. As for the genuineness of this scroll, I think there can be little doubt."

"Thank you, Professor. We will not trouble you to stay while we have our negotiations, but we will contact you to supervise any further study of the scroll. I'm sure I can rely on your confidentiality." The elderly Professor stood up, smiled and nodded to Saint-Saens and his guests before leaving the room.

"So, we are dealing with a very valuable document indeed, the earliest evidence about Jesus, I would suggest, and therefore worth a king's ransom," said L'Matin in a business-like voice. "Shall we start the negotiation at $50 million USD?"

Saint-Saens gasped and said, "Tres cher!! Monsieur L'Matin, that is a price certainly beyond our means! May I suggest something more like $25 million?"

"I am quite certain the British museum would outbid that offer," countered Henri.

Saint-Saens was beginning to get nervous. Perhaps L'Matin had already contacted other museums? In that case it would be wise to strike while the iron was hot and before a bidding war began. "Suppose we settle for $35 million then, surely a generous offer?"

"Not generous enough. I will take no less than $40 million for this object. My appraisers say it is worth up to $100 million, but since I want to keep doing business with you, I will give you a considerable discount."

Saint-Saens knew that L'Matin was a no nonsense kind of businessman, and that he had come to his bottom price. It was take it or leave it at this point. "Well, Monsieur L'Matin, this will prevent us from acquiring some other things we are bidding on even as I speak, but in the name of compromise I will accept your price. I have taken the liberty to have a deed of title and contract drawn up, so we may finalize the negotiation now. As before, we will transfer the funds into your Banque Nationale d'Paris account immediately. Will that be satisfactory?"

And so it was that the scroll dug up in Capernaum became the latest prized possession of the Louvre.

At precisely four o'clock, Pierre Saint-Saens stood up behind a podium in the press room of the museum, tapped the microphone and said, "My assistant will now distribute a press release for your use as you write your stories. I will read the initial paragraph of the release and then take questions."

> The Louvre, the greatest repository of antiquities and art in the world, is pleased to announce that it has acquired one of the most rare and precious documents yet found by archaeologists. This document is clearly from the first or early second century A.D. and is likely the earliest Christian document of any kind. It contains a collection of Jesus' own sayings in early Aramaic, the language which Jesus himself spoke. We will henceforth refer to this scroll as *The Gospel of Jesus*. Today is the day we draw as close as we can to the original words and teachings of Jesus.

There was a stunned silence among the some fifty people who had been allowed into the Louvre for this press conference. One reporter immediately raised a hand and asked, "Are you at liberty to tell us how the Louvre acquired this document and will it not be subject to extradition by the Israeli government since they have had a law since 1977 saying that no precious antiquity can leave their country?"

"We have legally bought this document from a well-known antiquities dealer who in turn bought it from another antiquities dealer. We have gone through proper and legal channels and our signed deed of title with the seller is such that our own lawyers are certain that no law of another country can supersede French law when it comes to objects *legally bought here in France*. This scroll was bought right here in Paris."

Another hand went up, "When will this great find go on display?"

"We plan to have a reception, by invitation only, on Saturday to inaugurate the opening of The Jesus Gospel exhibition."

The questions went on for another thirty minutes, but most of the reporters needed to get out of the room and call their editors to hold the presses for this big news. Saint-Saens watched his audience begin to scurry like rats, and he said to himself, "This is the greatest coup of my career. Nothing could top this. The reaction is going to be colossal."

Sammy Cohen was sitting in his office fretting over the police investigation of his missing scroll. The six o'clock news came on the small TV sitting on the edge of his desk. Sammy's head immediately jerked up when he heard . . .

> *Topping our news with this late-breaking story, it has just been announced that the Gospel of Jesus has been found, an ancient scroll in Aramaic in the original words of Jesus. The scroll has been acquired by the Louvre. A "by invitation only" gala will be held Saturday to unveil the document.*

"This can't be happening again! First the Lazarus stone and now our precious Q document! Sammy pressed the intercom button calling his secretary, who never left before he did, and screamed, "Get me the police—and get me Interpol! The missing Q document has turned up in France!"

35

THE HONEYMOON IS OVER

THEIR BEACH LIFE IN Antalya had come to an end and it was a time to head back to Istanbul. Around 7 AM Art kissed his sleepy bride and said, "Remember, we planned to drive to Ephesus this morning before going back to Istanbul. I want to revisit the House of Mary briefly before I talk to the Patriarch. And I really need more pictures of the Terrace Houses to go along with my study of magic in Ephesus. If we get going by 8, we should be in Ephesus by 2."

"More pictures?" teased Marissa. "You remind me of your shutterbug friend, Mark Fairchild."

"A master with a camera! But every picture I have of Mark shows him taking a picture of something else! By the way, he's providing all the photos for my New Testament textbook."

Marissa realized it was time to move on after lying on the beach, discussing baby options, deciding to get a nice, two-bedroom apartment in Istanbul, hashing over finances, and the like. They now sounded like a properly married couple.

Art headed down to the news stand to get the latest *Herald-Tribune*, the primary international English language newspaper. As he carried Marissa's Turkish coffee up the stairs into the hotel, one of the headlines stopped him dead in his tracks, the hot coffee spilling on his leg.

"Ouch!" he cried as he read, "GOSPEL OF JESUS ARRIVES IN PARIS."

Racing through the article, it dawned on Art that this was surely the scroll that Grace had been talking about. He made a mental note to call Grace, although she probably had her hands full right now.

Marissa had just slipped on a flower print blouse and was combing her long auburn hair when Art arrived. "You know, you would look beautiful in anything, and that's a fact. You could wear a burka and look beautiful. Ah, but then I couldn't see your new auburn tresses!"

"Well, thank you! I hope you feel the same when I'm old and gray!"

"That might happen sooner than you think. This story is bound to give us both a few gray hairs!" said Art as he waved the *Tribune* in the air.

Marissa grabbed the paper out of Art's hand and devoured the long article along with her coffee. Her eyes popping, she looked up at Art and said, "Why do I have a funny feeling this is the very thing you were talking to Grace about the other day?'

"Because it is—you being the good connector of the dots."

"And I suppose this means we need to go to Paris or Jerusalem or somewhere?'

"That will be entirely for us to decide. I admit I do want to talk to Grace at some point. For now, I'm proposing nothing except a scenic drive over the hills to Ephesus today followed by one more night at the Sea Pines in Kushadasi, and a flight back to Istanbul from Izmir tomorrow. In short, I'm not changing our plans! Are you with me?"

"Now and forever!" beamed Marissa. "Best put on your good walking shoes and not those flip flops." And with that, Art and Marissa took the elevator down to the lobby, checked out, and drove off into the morning sun.

~

Art and Marissa agreed that Ephesus is the perfect example of how to do

an archaeological dig properly. The terraced houses are perched on the slope next to the Library of Celsus right in the middle of downtown Ephesus on Curetes Street. What struck Art on this visit was the beauty of the frescoes and inlaid floors. These houses were more than a little colorful.

"The notion that the ancients were stodgy old dudes in white robes who had little appreciation for color is certainly given the lie at places like Ephesus and Pompeii. Look at those bright crimsons!" enthused Marissa. "I could look at this wall for a very long time and not get tired of it."

"The construction is interesting too—painted plaster panels on top of typical Roman bricks or stones," replied Art as he started taking pictures. "One has to wonder what the ancients actually thought about the mytho-logical figures and scenes that were painted in their houses. Was this like when I was a boy and had wallpaper with baseball players on it? I wouldn't want anyone to think that just because their pictures were on my wall, I was worshipping them," said Art in mock horror.

"And just look at that indoor plumbing—no outhouses or public fa-cilities for the über-wealthy here," laughed Marissa.

"It seems clear to me that time after time we underestimate the degree of sophistication of the ancients. You look at some of their engineering and architectural achievements and it's stunning compared to the rubbish we tend to construct. Our highways last about five years in a hot climate; some of those Roman roads can still be used 2,000 years later."

"You are so right, husband of mine. Archaeological work is humbling because you see how many skills we have lost over the centuries. Not many could do these frescoes and wall paintings today," added Marissa.

"That reminds me to show you the frescoes done by Ben Long that hang in various churches and buildings in Charlotte," promised Art.

The couple spent a happy couple of hours at the terrace houses where they ran into Professor Marmara who was also in charge of the cave church of Paul and Thecla. He offered to take them over to the House of Mary and

then to lead them on a little hike up Nightingale Mountain to see one of the earliest cave churches.

"We think pilgrims have been coming here since at least the second century. Early Christianity survived in the age of persecution often by going underground or in caves. Look at these 6th century frescoes—the only pictures of Paul we have here in Ephesus. Of course, you're looking at the most famous one—which also shows his female disciple, Thecla."

"My work hasn't involved reading about Thecla," admitted Marissa.

"That's not surprising," said the Professor. "We only know about Thecla, supposedly a young virgin, from a second century document called The Acts of Paul and Thecla. Her desire to remain a virgin got her into all sorts of trouble leading to miraculous escapes from death. It's quite the exciting read! She is revered for spreading the Gospel in those early days. You'll notice in the picture that Paul's image is intact, but Thecla's image has been vandalized!"

"Let me guess," said Marissa. "Someone didn't like the idea of Thecla being a witness for Jesus."

"Exactly! Some things never change. Women still struggle for the right to speak freely about their faith," said the archaeologist.

From the hillside cave, they looked over the city of Ephesus spread out in the valley below. They descended in silence. It was late when Marissa and Art arrived at their hotel in Kushadasi, but a good time to again watch the sunset over the Aegean.

36

THE RACE TO GAZA

ABDULLAH/SAUL WAS FEELING INCREASINGLY uneasy about staying on at the IAA, and so he resolved to quietly resign first thing Wednesday morning. Abdullah had already handed over Omar's money to the Hamas leadership. The local police interviewed Saul, and he believed he had passed for now, but he knew they were suspiciously considering the theft as at least in part an inside job. "Don't leave town," was their advice. But the plan was for Abdullah to be taken by a Hamas driver to Gaza later in the morning.

It was a humid June morning, even in the Judean hills where Jerusalem was located. Abdullah was already sweating. Sammy's secretary motioned him to a seat. From there he could see through the glass door that Sammy was on the phone with someone and the conversation was animated.

"Alright, I understand. So what you're saying is that there is nothing to be done immediately about the Louvre having the document. Your people will go look at the contracts and deed of title first? Well I guess that's a start. Thank you, *shalom*." Sammy slammed down the phone, went to the door, and motioned Saul to come in.

Still pacing around his office, Sammy said, "You may not have seen the news last night. The document has been found—in Paris! The Louvre paid a lot of shekels for that document I presume. At least one someone is very wealthy today!"

"No!" replied Saul quite honestly for a change. "I certainly had not heard this! You say the document is at the Louvre!? Then surely you can get it back!"

"It's not that simple. The police will try to track down the paper trail, of course, but right now, ownership is nine tenths of the law! I'm sure the Louvre does not want to part with the document, and their insurance people don't want to pay out!"

Still worrying about the investigation but putting on his best sad face, Saul said, "Dr. Cohen, I owe you a lot for hiring me for this job, but I think it's time you get somebody who does a better job. I'm resigning effective now. As you know, I feel terrible about this theft, and it will take a while, God willing, for me to get over it."

Sammy looked at Saul sympathetically and replied, "We all come up short sometime, but I'm sure you did your best. You were up against a professional criminal apparently. Are you sure I can't persuade you to stay?"

"I'm afraid not. I come to work feeling like I failed. I need to move on." Sammy extended his hand. Saul shook it and turned to go.

"Thank you for your service, albeit brief. I have your street address and I'll just send the check there." As soon as he left, Sammy called the police. He had been instructed to "play dumb" with Saul who was now a prime suspect.

As Saul got to his small brown car, he was so deep in thought that he didn't notice the unmarked blue car parked on the other side of the little circle drive. Nor was he paying attention when the blue car followed him as he headed out.

When Abdullah finally parked and went into *Fatma's Laundry* on the top of the Mount of Olives, the Israeli antiquities police had no reason to think he wouldn't come out the way he had gone in. He seemed to be in no hurry, and he was carrying a bundle of clothes under his arm.

The shop itself led to an alley at the back, where a "runner" was parked in a black Mercedes. His job was to ferry Hamas people back and forth from Gaza, going through Jericho and then south through the desert before turning towards the coast. This involved driving on gravel tracks once followed by camels and spice merchants, but it was the only way to get to Gaza undetected, except for the "eye in the sky" watching this whole area from the air.

When Abdullah did not come out of the shop after thirty minutes, Tevi went in to see what was keeping the man, only to discover he was nowhere to be found and the woman behind the counter claimed she didn't know the man when shown his picture. Tevi shouted to his partner, "We've been duped. He's on the run!"

Hamas had been making these secret journeys for many years, and now that the Fatah party had made peace with Hamas in a ceremony in Egypt, there was more co-operation between the West bank Palestinians and the Gaza Palestinians. Hamas had assigned their best driver, Mohamar, to this task of rescuing Abdullah who had faithfully brought Hamas millions in much needed cash.

The Mercedes circumnavigated the Israeli checkpoints by going through back roads and alleys, until the car came out on the Jericho road. The driver had been warned that the usual checkpoints were on alert, and he was taking no chances. Abdullah sat in the back seat, sweating with his stomach in knots. What would happen now to his family in east Jerusalem? Would he ever see them again? These were the questions he asked after being brave for Hamas. Perhaps he could persuade his family to move to the Gaza safe house.

Speeding past two Bedouin camps on the side of the road, the sun beat down on the front hood of the car, and the glare was fierce. Once in Jericho, the car took a dramatic right turn onto a dirt track heading past the Monastery of St. George and on into the desert. Then turning east again the car began the long journey down to Gaza and the coast. In the distance the driver could hear the sound of a helicopter. Doubtless a Mercedes speeding through this part of the desert would attract attention.

"We've been spotted," said Mohamar. "Be prepared for a bumpy ride the rest of the way," he yelled back to Abdullah. Despite his work in the security profession, Abdullah was not made of stone, and he had a propensity for carsickness if riding in the back of a car on a windy road. Rolling down the window, he vomited on the side of the car and felt a little better.

"Here, have some cold water," growled Mohamar as he pitched back a plastic bottle.

The helicopter was now close enough to read the license plate through binoculars. "It's a good thing we have Israeli plates. Perhaps they will think we're on some Mosad mission taking someone out into the desert to dispose of them," laughed Mohamar.

In fact, the plates were stolen from an old, seemingly abandoned car in Tel Aviv belonging to one Camelia Levine, Grace's mother! Though she died the previous year, Grace had not gotten around to selling the car that was parked at a garage where Grace regularly got her car serviced.

In the helicopter the man riding shotgun radioed headquarters. "I've got a fix on the Israeli license plate." He waited briefly for them to run the plate. "Say what? This car belongs to a little old lady in Tel Aviv? Well, she's driving like a maniac across the desert about now. See if you can't get me more info!"

Because there was no confirmation, the Mercedes had made good progress through the back roads and was now less than a mile from the backdoor of Gaza. Suddenly the microphone squawked at the second man in the helicopter, and his contact at headquarters said, "The plates are stolen. It was reported last week. We don't know who's in that car, but you might want to think about trying to stop them before they get to Gaza. Obviously they are driving like a bat out of hell for a reason."

The pilot of the helicopter had heard this song before. "Let's strafe them a little bit. Maybe they'll stop."

The car was now five minutes from the Gaza checkpoint. The helicopter buzzed the car firing over its top. Mohamar yelled, "Get down Abdullah, get down!" So frightened was the driver that he didn't bother to stop at the gate. He rammed right through and raced into an alley that led to the main square in Gaza.

In a sarcastic voice he said to his passenger who was now on the floor in the backseat, "Welcome to the garden spot known as Gaza. We hope you have enjoyed your journey."

37

THE PRESS CONFERENCE

GRACE LEVINE HAD MIXED feelings about this press conference. On the one hand, the initial data from the Q document deserved an airing. On the other hand, having a press conference just made Sammy Cohen and the IAA look incompetent. Fidgeting with her notes, Grace peered out from behind the curtain in the lecture hall at Hebrew University. There were perhaps one hundred people sitting in a 500-seat auditorium, and Grace wondered why. Why had the Lazarus stone generated so much more interest than this Aramaic document? Wasn't Jesus hot news anymore? Grace was puzzled. Perhaps the press conference had occurred too quickly for the international media to show up.

Sammy Cohen was ready to introduce Grace. Looking over at her, he sighed. She looked fabulous in her navy business suit and red heels. He still wished he could have won the courting battle. As Sammy walked across the stage, the flashes from the cameras were noticeable but not overwhelming.

When he reached the podium, someone yelled out, "Why can't our IAA hold on to our own treasures?" This produced an awkward pause.

Sammy just went on. "I am pleased to inform you that despite the theft of the Q document, we know where it is—at the Louvre in Paris. I mention this not to provide more fodder for unnecessary jibes, but so you will realize that when Professor Levine talks to you about this document it is on the basis that: 1) there is a genuine document carefully authenticated now in two countries; 2) we know it came from a dig at Capernaum led by our own Rami Arav; and 3) the authenticity of the original document is not in question—our photocopies are identical.

"Efforts are underway to recover our stolen property and apprehend the thief. In the meantime, I am pleased to introduce Professor Grace Levine, chair of the Biblical Languages division at Hebrew University, and one of the world's top experts in ancient Aramaic inscriptions. Please welcome Professor Levine."

Grace looked into the crowd while the flashbulbs popped, and noticed the long-haired young man sitting on the second row. Grayson was eager to hear what his mentor had to say about the Q document.

Clearing her throat, Grace looked into the cameras and began. "For well over a century, scholars have hypothesized that there must be a document or some oral sources that account for the considerable degree of identical content in Matthew and Luke, which is not found in Mark. Of course, there were scholars who wanted to urge that this overlap of some 250 plus verses could be accounted for on the theory that Matthew used Luke or vice versa, but these two theories had serious weaknesses, not least of which is that Matthew had material that Luke would have been itching to get his hands on, and vice versa. The theory then of the First or Third Evangelists borrowing from their counterpart's Gospel never quite explained things.

"The theory of a Q document, Q for the German word *Quelle* which means source, has been bandied about for decades and decades. But there was no tangible evidence of such a document. Then, when the Gospel of Thomas was discovered, the theory gained more traction because that document mostly contains sayings of Jesus with no Passion or Resurrection stories, indeed with very little narrative material of any kind. It presents us with a 'Jesus the talking head' rather than a 'Jesus the worker of miracles' and the like. However, the Gospel of Thomas appears to come from Syria and from the latter part of the second century. It reflects knowledge of not merely the material in Matthew, Mark, Luke and some of John, but even the final editing of those documents. In short, it could not have arisen before those Gospels. So, we were still left with the following question—Was there an early written collection of Jesus' sayings, earlier than the written canonical Gospels?

"In my view, we can now answer that question with a great big YES! I say this after studying the contents of this newly found scroll. First of all, the document is in Aramaic, and it is the Aramaic of the right period. Secondly, since the document is in Aramaic, and the Gospels are in Greek, we can say that here we are closer to the original sayings of Jesus. In translating Aramaic into Greek there are always various possibilities, and so one of the theories I entertained first was that perhaps Matthew and Luke independently translated this Q material in their own ways. This would account for the differences in the Sermon on the Mount and the Lord's Prayer. The problem with this thesis is that Luke does not seem to know Aramaic. He eliminates all the Aramaic phrases from his Markan source. So another theory is required.

"For a moment let's consider what Papias said about Matthew. Here I quote Papias: 'Matthew put together the oracles [of the Lord] in the Hebrew language, and each one interpreted them as best he could.' Notice two things about this quote. First of all, the phrase 'in the Hebrew language' might be rendered 'in the Semitic tongue'. Non-Hebrew speakers like Papias often equated Hebrew with its cousin Aramaic, and vice versa. So Papias could well mean Aramaic, the Semitic daily language of Jesus. The second thing to note is that it says Matthew himself put together the *logia* of Jesus which probably means sayings—the sayings of Jesus in the Semitic tongue he spoke. Now we are getting somewhere. The verb 'put together' suggests he collected and assembled the sayings of Jesus. I think we now have confirmation of what Papias was saying. The Q document comes from a disciple who had contact with some of the original eyewitnesses of Jesus.

"I'm convinced that the person who produced this document was a professional scribe, and an Aramaic expert to boot. And remember, this scroll was found in Capernaum. I stress this because 1) Matthew was a tax collector and a literate scribe who could write documents; and 2) Matthew operated in Capernaum!"

At this moment, Grayson was heard to blurt out, "How cool is that?!"

Grace smiled and continued, "What I suggest is that Papias was not referring to a Gospel, as he does when he talks about Mark's work. When he mentions Matthew he is referring to the very document that we are now talking about—the Q or Jesus scroll. It is possible that Matthew also assembled a Gospel based on Mark and this Q scroll and some independent traditions, but that is a discussion for another day.

"I suggest that we have a pre-Gospel document, and as such its major significance is that it gets us closer to the original words of Jesus than we have ever been before! We can now hear the original voice of Jesus!"

At this point she spent the next few minutes reading the Aramaic of the Lord's Prayer. "What you have just heard is the most famous Jewish prayer in human history in its mother tongue—the so-called Lord's Prayer, though it might better be called the disciple's prayer, since it is one Jesus gave to his disciples to use.

"I can now say that the Q material in Matthew's Gospel is closer to this Aramaic original of the sayings of Jesus than Luke's version. We already knew that the First Evangelist was a rather conservative editor of his source material. For example, he takes over 95% of the material he found in Mark, and of that 95% the verbatim rate is about 52%, a very conservative approach to a use of an ancient source. We might hypothesize just on the basis of this data, that he would be conservative in the way he handled the Q material as well, and I can now say that appears definitely to be the case. Though Q specialists tend to suggest that the Lukan form of Q sayings is more original than the Matthean ones, we now have evidence to the contrary.

"Note that we can no longer say that the sayings of Jesus went through a long process of oral passing on of the material before it was written down. No, we now have evidence that this is not likely so. Matthew composed this document very early on, perhaps as early as the 40s when the Christian community was really taking off in Capernaum. Here we have a window behind the Gospels into the Jesus of history, and he looks very much like the Jesus who speaks in Matthew's Gospel, including the more messianic materials in Q. David Flusser, of blessed memory, was right that Jesus had a messianic self-understanding and was in various ways a unique Jew. We may not choose or wish to pledge our own faith in that Jesus, but it seems no longer possible to deny he had a messianic self-understanding.

"Finally, I want to share something I discovered just yesterday. These 500 lines are divided up into five or six sections. Each section is a continuous flow of letters without punctuation, without sentence division, without paragraphing, and yea verily without chapters and verses. But what I noticed is that an older conjecture of Professor Arthur West appears to be correct. Q was arranged in such a way to present Jesus as a sage, a man wiser than Moses, hence we have not only the Sermon on the Mount, but five or six divisions in this document. But in this document's structure Jesus is also presented as one greater than Solomon, the ultimate sage and son of David. These matters will need further study at length, but they are suggestive."

"Let me sum up the most important point. We can no longer say that we are several steps removed from the voice of Jesus. I see little reason to doubt that the compiler of this document simply collected and wrote down sayings of Jesus in the original language. This after all was the job of a scribe copying a source—to record it as nearly verbatim as he could, but then to frame the material in ways that produced new insights.

"Today we find ourselves closer to the voice of Jesus than at any point since the first century. Let us all heed Jesus' admonition, 'Let those with two good ears, hear!'"

The applause rang out until Grace raised her hand. "And now a few questions."

A man wearing a *NY Times* badge said, "Are you saying that we now have evidence that people like the Jesus Seminar folks are wrong about the percentage of authentic sayings of Jesus in a Gospel like Matthew's?"

"Yes, that is one implication. This may come as a surprise, but in fact the Gospel writers appear to be rather conservative editors of their sources."

A woman from the *Jerusalem Post* asked, "Do you think it's time for us to set up a study center here in Jerusalem to study the teachings of Jesus?"

"That is exactly what I would like to see happen. It's high time more Jews and Christians studied the teachings of Jesus the Jew together."

"Were there any big surprises? Any new revelations about Jesus?" asked Grayson.

"There is one thing. Matthew 11:25–27 has often been thought to be later theologizing about Jesus. But apparently this is not so. Apparently Jesus really did say something like 'only the Son knows the Father' and vice versa. Jesus seems to have had a clear sense that he needed to reveal God to Jews in a way others couldn't. And interestingly the use of the term *Abba* [Father] for God is all over this document."

The time had flown by, and as Grace excused herself, Grayson came up to her and said, "Sign me up for the Jesus study center!"

Grace smiled. "I figured you'd want in on the ground floor. But first we need to plan a smaller symposium. And you're just the newly minted Ph.D to do that! Maybe we can get Art West to join us eventually."

"I'll start praying about that! Maybe Abba will persuade him!" beamed Grayson.

Grace walked off the platform with Sammy. Almost immediately, Grace's phone rang. "Grace! Art and Marissa calling! We watched your press conference on my computer. I do hope to help you in any way I can!"

Suddenly Marissa butted in. "Of course, he's not going anywhere without me so you and Manny had better be prepared for company down the road."

"Excellent! Now you two need to get back to the honeymoon. What kind of couple huddles around a laptop to watch a geek on a small screen talk about academic stuff? "

"Two archaeology buffs, that's who!" laughed Marissa.

Art added, "We are flying from Izmir back to Istanbul late today. It's hard to tell when the honeymoon really ends and 'real life' begins. I know we plan to get a small flat in Istanbul—Marissa's studio loft won't cut it for long. But we will see you soon, I'm sure of it."

38

THE FRETTING PATRIARCH

BARTHOLOMEW WAS NOT USED to waiting. Since becoming the Patriarch, people and things were at his beck and call. Only this time because of a wedding and a honeymoon he was abiding his soul in patience in regard to consulting with Professor West about the Mary debacle. He kept muttering to himself, patience is a virtue, patience is a virtue. Sitting in his office behind a huge polished mahogany desk, the Patriarch was about to deal with the endless paperwork confronting him when the large red phone on his desk rang.

"Your Eminence, there is a man on the line from the local police. Shall I put him through?" asked his secretary.

"Yes please," said the Patriarch, his curiosity aroused.

"Patriarch, this is Inspector Oguz and I have some news for you. We've been able to trace the cyanide used to kill the priests. It appears to have been bought in a shop in the Galata district here in Istanbul—not legally of course. We are talking with the shop owner."

"Thank you for keeping me informed. Of course, if there's anything I can do for you, let me know."

"Naturally, but I do have a word of warning for you. I suggest you tighten up security. And I wouldn't trust anyone—not even your staff. Information is easily obtained—for a price. Two clerics are dead—there's no reason why you wouldn't also be a target again. It was just two months ago that we uncovered an assassination plot! Have your security check on the kitchen staff again—cyanide or arsenic can easily be added. I'm not suggesting a "food taster" but be careful. I do suggest that you not leave Istanbul anytime soon. I will call you again when I have more info," promised Inspector Oguz before he hung up.

Now the Patriarch began to fret about his staff—anyone could be suspect. And then there was the matter of the House of Mary. Few people knew about the find, but could he trust them not to leak the information? Father Nikodemos, the only priest besides himself that knew about the Mary matter, was overseeing the work at the House of Mary. But there were workers and lab technicians and a host of others who all had some contact with the excavations, the crypt, and the corpse. Time for another long chat with Father Nikodemos he concluded.

But the phone rang again, startling him considerably. "Your eminence, Doctor Arthur West is on the line. Shall I put him through?" asked Diana, his secretary.

"Absolutely!" replied the Patriarch. "And afterwards put Father Nikodemos on speed dial!" Then he heard Art's voice.

"Your Eminence, my wife and I are returning to Istanbul late today. We are hoping to meet with you in regard to the finds at the House of Mary. Just yesterday we were in Ephesus with Professor Marmara. We had time to make a brief visit to the House. I wish now that I had arranged for a longer visit with your archaeology team."

"This is good news, Dr. West. I am eager to re-examine the find through your eyes. And yes, a special tour can be arranged for you both. Father Nikodemos is supervising the project. His office is nearby in Selchuk. Fortunately for us here on the western side of Turkey Ephesus is not so far off!"

"Yes, it is convenient, and there is so much to do and see in Ephesus—it remains my favorite archaeological site! Are you planning a trip to Ephesus anytime soon?" asked Art.

"I should, but apparently the authorities are a bit worried about me. With the deaths of two clerics, my life is also in question."

"Didn't I read about an assassination plot recently?"

"Unfortunately, yes. But let us talk about more happy things. I trust your honeymoon has gone well?"

"Thank you for asking. We toured and we relaxed. But I think we both need to get back to the real world—if archaeology can be considered the real world!"

The Patriarch laughed. "It is good to stop working and enjoy life a bit. But if you enjoy your work, all the better! I look forward to working with you both."

And on that note the Patriarch ended the conversation. For a moment, he felt a little better and vowed to pray to stop worrying so much and let God take charge.

39

A SAFE HOUSE?

IT HAD BEEN A day now since Abdullah's escape to Gaza, and while he was beginning to relax, the reality of it all was setting in. He was now a fugitive from Israeli justice, and those folks were mad, very mad. So mad they might even be prepared to swap hostages with Hamas to catch this thief. As Abdullah feared, Mosad had figured out that the theft of the Jesus scroll was an inside job, and the only insider who fit the profile was Saul Levi, except Saul Levi was a dead man!

~

At this precise moment, Detective Weinstein was sitting in the office of Sammy Cohen. "I'm sorry to tell you that your security guard was not Saul Levi, but an agent of Hamas sent precisely to steal things and fill up Hamas' coffers. We are not sure yet who he is, but we are pretty sure he escaped to Gaza just a couple of days ago."

Sammy sighed. "Saul came with a good reference from a rabbi and seemed like a very reliable person. It's a mystery. If he did steal the scroll, then why did he stay around?"

"It's called hiding in plain sight. This is a good way to throw the scent off your own trail. By the way, Saul wasn't the only person in the building at the time of the crime—you were too!! But before you start calling your lawyer, you're not a suspect! Just leave it at that! However, I suggest you let the professionals do your background checks in the future. We have his photo ID, so it shouldn't take long to track him—if he's in the system. We'll keep you posted," said the Detective as he rose to go.

⁓

Abdullah sat down at the computer in the safe house and typed in his email address. In light of how volatile things were in Gaza and how his deed was drawing more attention to Gaza authorities, Abdullah was thinking he should go even further away, and then send for his family. He had two choices, Jordan or Egypt, Jordan being less volatile than Egypt at the moment. He typed out the following message to his wife.

"*Salam aleichum*. I am safe in Gaza. We should move to Jordan. I long to be back with you and the children. Abdullah."

⁓

Facial recognition software found no match for the photo ID. "Who is this guy?" muttered Detective Weinstein. He was now resorting to local mug shots—a couple of hundred with no luck.

"This is a needle in a haystack," he muttered again. "Let's try altering the photo—add a mustache, add a beard, add hair for that matter! Palestinians, if he is Palestinian, are not usually bald!"

Finally, the computer listed a few potential matches, but age wise the best bet was one Abdullah Hashimi who lived in east Jerusalem. Weinstein noted the address down, and then cross-checked to see if Hashimi had any police record at all. He did not, not even a parking ticket, but that didn't mean he was clean. Hamas operatives are smart enough to fly under the radar. He called his partner. "Let's take a ride!"

40

MATERNAL INSTINCTS

JOYCE SAT ON THE porch as her realtor led one group of potential buyers after another through her home. She had very mixed feelings. On the one hand, she did want to move home to Wilmington. On the other hand, this house had so many good memories. It was hard to leave all that behind. Fortunately, Laura was still in the States, albeit traveling about raising money for the orphanage.

Jake was still coming and going frequently even though the basketball season was over. His Hornets had made the playoffs, barely, but had been bounced in the first round by the mighty Chicago Bulls. Now that the wedding was over, Jake was spending time at the Bethlehem Community Center playing hoops with under-privileged children and planning a summer camp. And there were four hour trips to Wilmington to see Melody, his fiancée, who was hoping to finish her degree in December by taking summer classes. His plan was to move to a condo in downtown Charlotte. He and Melody wanted to start planning their wedding for next summer.

As people filed through, Joyce mulled over the conversation she had with James Howell the previous afternoon. She unburdened her worries about Art and Marissa—worries about their safety, worries about their future, and worries about grandchildren not even born yet!

"How do you pray about a bad feeling?" she asked.

"Pray for protection; pray that God will guide their decisions. And promise me you'll leave the decision about children entirely in God's hands! They've got enough on their plate!" said James with a frown.

"But a mother worries!" countered Joyce.

"I hate to sound sexist, but your maternal instincts are in overdrive!" insisted James. "Let go and let God!"

"But I haven't heard from him in days!" she moaned.

"Days! You are fortunate to have heard anything at all! He's a good son to keep in touch even weekly during his honeymoon. Count your blessings," advised James. "And most importantly, remember that worrying is counterproductive. I'm not saying, don't worry, be happy. I'm saying, don't worry, just pray. Put that worrying time to better use. Pray without ceasing!"

"Now you are really making sense," smiled Joyce who left James' office in a much better frame of mind.

The older she had gotten the more vulnerable she felt about herself and her family. Emails were no substitute for phone calls, in her mind, but emails were better than nothing. She had to admit, both Laura and Art emailed frequently by most peoples' standards.

Taking a deep breath she smiled as Donna her real estate agent came over and said, "Looks like we have someone who wants to make an offer. Can we talk over lunch?"

"That would be great," said Joyce. "Let's go to McCormick and Schmick's which is just over at South Park."

"Okay, but give me another fifteen minutes to wrap up this house tour."

"Thank you for letting me sit on the porch during the open house," said Joyce with a wistful smile. She was going to miss this place.

~

Grace had been dying to see Hannah's son Samuel. The antiquities shop looked bright and clean thanks to Hannah. She had the place sanitized and baby proofed before Samuel was born. Despite having come into a considerable amount of money from the sale of a first-century menorah, Hannah and Kahlil still lived in the back of the shop. But Hannah had dreams of a new home—getting her father to move would be the problem.

Kahlil was just completing a sale of two pottery lamps to a dealer in the US. With Hannah's help, Kahlil had become rather proficient selling his goods over the internet. He smiled when the doorbell tinkled and waved Grace through as he continued to wheel and deal.

Grace could hear Hannah talking to Samuel in a high voice like Moms often do. She was now well past the horrible events of her assault, and somehow God had turned even that into a blessing.

"Aunt Grace is here, and look what I brought—a book about a little boy living in Jerusalem!"

Hannah came over from the play pen and hugged Grace. "It's so good of you to come what with your busy schedule! I heard about the conference this morning on the news at noon. I can't believe you could find time to stop by and see us today!"

"What are you talking about? I wouldn't miss a meeting with a prophet like Samuel for all the press conferences in the world. This is the stuff that really makes the world go around—parents and children."

When Grace said this she was suddenly overcome with emotion. Though she had no children of her own, she was so glad to now have Yelena in her life. And as a bonus, she got to be a surrogate Aunt! Today was her day to enjoy that. Since she had adopted Yelena as a teenager, she never had the joy of dealing with infants or toddlers. Her time with Hannah and Samuel made up for that.

"Here, you hold Samuel for a bit. He's just been fed so don't jiggle him too much," laughed Hannah. "He can crawl with the best of them, and he's trying to walk already. I really wanted to have a better home for him. I've just got to get my father to move. We have lived in these back rooms all our lives!"

"My Mother was eager to move to Tel Aviv because she knew she would be near us. She didn't live that long but she enjoyed her time. I wish she could have met Yelena. Maybe your Father will realize that the people are more important than the house," suggested Grace.

"I can tell how nervous he gets when I bring it up, but it's time for us to move."

"Show him places where his grandson can have lots of space to run and play."

"My instincts just tell me that we should move—there are good memories here, but some very bad ones also."

"I agree. You need a fresh start with your son."

Kahlil had been listening to the conversation and realized that for both of these women their maternal instincts were in high gear. And he knew Hannah's instincts were strong and true. The shop would stay, but his family should move.

41

HIT AND RUN

ART HAD JUST FINISHED two phone calls, one to Grace and the other to the Patriarch. He was staring at a long line of emails on his computer. Marissa was still packing, but she decided to go for a short run on the beach before they had lunch and headed off to the airport in Izmir. From the window she could tell that the beach was already filling up with tourists. To herself she said, "Funny how I think of everyone else as a tourist, but not myself." Maybe it was because this was her country, and most of the people who spent their holidays in Izmir were not Turkish. They preferred less commercial places like Chesme or Foca. Marissa quickly put on her bathing suit, running shorts, white socks and running shoes.

She waved to Art who just nodded his head as she headed out the door. For a moment she lingered at the coffee shop to glance at the newspaper headlines, didn't see anything interesting, and so continued to the main boulevard which led eventually past the Migros, the local supermarket, to the beach itself.

Aziz was drinking mid-morning coffee in front of his hotel, and hiding behind his newspaper. He had been keeping the Circle of Five well informed, but they were getting anxious for him to come back to Istanbul. He had accomplished nothing so far on his wild goose chase.

When he looked up and saw Marissa go by, all alone, he realized his window of opportunity was at hand. She seemed unaware that he was following her.

Marissa was in no hurry. She stopped frequently to look in the shop windows. Eventually, she reached the beach and started a slow jog towards the more isolated inlet. Her ear buds and favorite tunes shut out the world. She was lost in her thoughts about life as a wife.

Rounding the bend that led into the inlet, Marissa did not see the man who tackled her from behind. As she fell into the sand, she attempted to turn over but failed. Suddenly her arms were pinned to the ground by a pair of strong legs. She attempted again to roll over, to kick him in the groin, but quickly he forced a smelly rag into her mouth. And then her vision dimmed and all went black when he hit her head with a rock. Aziz left Marissa where she was since he saw no one else on the beach, and ran back to the parking lot behind the little coffee shop, jumped in his car, slammed his foot on the accelerator, and drove down to the access road where he had assaulted Marissa. Backing his car up to the end of the access road, Aziz dragged Marissa's limp body to the car and dumped it into the trunk. Her cell phone fell out of her pocket. He threw it on the ground and crushed it beyond recognition. "That's what I should have done to her head," he thought. Then he called Iskender, leader of the Circle of Five.

"*Efendi*?" said the voice at the other end.

"It's Aziz, and I have some good news for you from Kushadasi! I caught the bird, the lady archaeologist, who is the new wife of Dr. West. I could kill her, but then it occurred to me she might be worth more to us alive than dead, so what do you suggest?"

The man coughed and said without a little surprise in his voice, "Aziz, it was wise for you to consult me! You are right. We may not get a king's ransom, but I am willing to bet West or someone will pay a lot of lira to get Marissa Okur back. So here is what you are going to do. You are going to pass my mobile number to West, with the warning that if he gives it out to anyone, say the police, he will endanger the life of his wife. I will set up a payment plan and a drop site for the money. I want you to drive to Izmir and lock the woman in Ekrem's empty apartment. The key is over the door. Stay with her! Don't let her out of your sight. Handcuff her to a pipe if you have to. But get out of Kushadasi. Am I clear!?"

There was a pause at the other end of the line. "I leave West the note, business to you, and drive to Izmir."

"Right. *Allah akbar*," said Iskender.

"*Allah akbar,*" replied Aziz. What Iskender had not considered was that there was hardly a place in Turkey where Marissa Okur had more contacts and friends than Izmir.

Art had been pouring over his emails until he realized that Marissa was still gone. How long had it been? Two hours? He tried her cell phone—no answer. She's probably just enjoying the beach and lost track of time. He decided to put some suitcases in the car, but he saw a note on the floor wedged under the door.

In bad English it read, "Welcome to bad nightmares. We have wife of yours. If you want to see her alive, you do what we want. No police. Call number at 7 P.M. sharp. Circle of Five." A Turkish number was scribbled at the bottom.

Art was shaking, and a cold chill ran up his spine. Should I call the police? Should I call her family? So many things ran through Art's mind. When you are a single person, when something bad happens to you, you may still be able to cope reasonably well. But when it happens to your new wife, you fall to pieces. And that was exactly what happened to Art. He went into the bathroom shaking badly and threw up what little contents were in his stomach. In the distance, thunder could be heard. Dark clouds were gliding over the sea toward Kushadasi. Art West felt that darkness seep into his very soul.

42

THE ISRAELIS CAN WAIT

Monsieur Saint-Saens slammed down the phone with a look of disgust on his face. Had Henri L'Matin really pulled a fast one on him, or had he actually bought the Jesus scroll from a reputable Middle Eastern antiquities dealer? Inquiring minds wanted to know. On the one hand, his lawyers seemed confident everything was legal. There was no 'extradition of stolen antiquities' agreement between Israel and France. But as Sammy Cohen had just reminded Saint-Saens, the Israeli Museum and the Louvre had often cooperated and there would be no more cooperation ever if something wasn't done about the theft of the Jesus scroll.

And then there was the French press. *Le Monde* printed a detailed story calling the finding and buying of this manuscript the "steal of the century" though they meant it more tongue in cheek than reality. *Le Figaro* ran a story about Jesus in the aftermath of the Da Vinci Code frenzy, and the tabloids went crazy saying that the new manuscript proved that Jesus was French—he couldn't stop talking, even about religion!

Pierre looked out his window at a beautiful June day with the birds chirping. A row of Lombardy poplars lined the sidewalk. An Italian Smart Car was trying to park in a space that would fit a motorcycle. He returned to his desk but turned up his nose at the half-eaten pastry and cold cup of coffee.

A folder, already stuffed with drawings, outlined plans for the grand opening of the "Gospel According to Jesus" exhibit. Every plan had been put aside to produce the exhibit. Every available worker in the Louvre was scurrying to make it happen this weekend. At this point he couldn't even contemplate giving the scroll back to Israel because he had invested too much of the Louvre's time and money in this purchase. His Board would never forgive him if he didn't both recoup the cost and save the Louvre from international embarrassment.

Sighing, he got up from behind his desk and walked out the door and over to the elevator. Pressing the up button he got off on the third floor where the special exhibit would be held, away from some of the other treasures like the Venus de Milo and the Mona Lisa. The Jesus scroll would have its own space, carefully guarded by an amazing amount of security, which in itself was expensive. But it would all be worth it, Saint-Saens told himself. He was already collecting some of the other less illustrious biblical manuscripts in the Louvre to include in this special exhibit. The Jesus scroll would take center stage in a sealed, bullet-proof, glass container.

Saint-Saens also wanted to offer a number of lecture series over the summer. He called on his American contacts who suggested some highly skilled Aramaic scholars. It wasn't difficult to entice them to come to Paris. Free room and board, a stipend, and a chance to study the Q document made for an offer they couldn't refuse.

One of these, Dr. William Arnold, was a close friend of Art West. He and his wife Susan were already looking forward to staying in an apartment near the Louvre for the month of July in exchange for William's expert commentary on Aramaic. He considered the invitation an unexpected honor.

Standing now in front of the manuscript itself, Saint-Saens marveled at its very existence. This was as close as anyone could get to the original voice of Jesus. This is what he sounded like and what he said. He would specifically ask Dr. Arnold to give public readings of the script in Aramaic. There was rhythm and rhyme and assonance and alliteration. Jesus was a poet, a Jewish poet. The French just loved this sort of thing—the sound of an exotic language. Saint-Saens remembered an exhibit a few years back where someone had come and read Kahlil Gibran's *The Prophet* in its original Lebanese. People had gone crazy buying recordings and French editions of the poetic book. This was going to happen all over again with this Jesus scroll, he was sure.

Just now Saint-Saens was mulling over who besides Arnold to get to do a critical edition coffee table book, offering a fresh translation of the sayings of Jesus from the Aramaic into English (because it was the worldwide language of the Internet), as well as into various European languages.

Perhaps that Jesus scholar Arthur West who had been to the Louvre before would be a good choice? He would think about it. West with all his TV work certainly drew a crowd.

Staring through the glass at line upon line of uninterrupted Aramaic characters without punctuation of any kind, Saint-Saens thought about the nature of an oral culture. What he was looking at was an oral text, a text one could only make sense of if read aloud, carefully separating the words by pronouncing everything. Perhaps a good lecture on oral cultures and their scribes and texts could be part of the lecture series. It was a good idea. Someone could talk about the levels of literacy in Jesus' day and how hearing was about the only way most people learned things, as they could not read or write.

Suddenly a walky-talky squawked on the belt of a nearby security guard and he approached the curator. "Monsieur Saint-Saens, you are wanted downstairs. It appears President Sarkozy himself and his wife have come for a private viewing of the Jesus scroll. I hope you were given advance notice."

"No, I wasn't!" said a perturbed Saint-Saens, but this was typical of French politicians. They thought they owned the Louvre. "I will go and meet them now." As he was riding down in the elevator, it dawned on him. This is but a harbinger of how big all this was going to be. A little smile crept across his wrinkled face and he said to himself, "The Israelis will just have to wait. I will figure something out."

43

ART'S AGONY

ART WASHED HIS FACE and looked in the bathroom mirror. He hardly recognized the disheveled looking man staring back at him. His life had just
gone from ecstasy to agony, and he was not at all sure what to do about it.
The note simply gave him a phone number to call at 7 P.M. Art was now
debating whether it would make things better or worse to call the police,
report the kidnapping, and give them the number. Whatever he did, he
did not want to endanger Marissa's life. He finally decided to call his friend
Levent in Izmir and seek his advice. Better not to alarm his family or the
Okurs just yet. What could they do at this point anyway?

The phone rang for what seemed like an eternity and finally Art heard
the voice of his long-time friend saying, "How can I help you?" Levent was
an extraordinary person. Well educated and handsome, he owned one of
the premier travel agencies that specializes in helping Christians visit their
holy sites in Turkey and beyond.

"Levent, this is Art."

"Your voice sounds strained, are you okay?"

"Actually no, I am not at all okay. Marissa has been kidnapped here in
Kushadasi and it looks like they are going to hold her for ransom. Honestly,
I'm at my wit's end, and feel helpless. I don't know what to do. All I have is
a phone number that I'm supposed to call tonight at 7. I was sure hoping
that you would have some wisdom for me. What should I do? I'm afraid
for Marissa. I'm afraid she will come unglued especially if this drags on for

weeks. Oh, one other thing. The note was signed the Circle of Five. Does that ring any bells?"

"Oh dear! They have been all over the news in the last several weeks. They are suspected of being the ones who killed those two Christian priests. They are a radical Islamic group who hate our secular democracy and Turkey's co-operation with the West."

"If that was supposed to comfort me, it didn't," replied Art, his eyes welling with tears. "You're telling me they are very, very dangerous to someone like me or Marissa. I have no idea where Marissa is being held, so I don't know if I should stay where I am or go back to Istanbul."

"Why don't you wait and see what the next phone call tells you. In the meantime all of us here at the office will be praying for you and for Marissa's safe release. Let's not call the police into this just yet. But if there is no good reason to stay where you are, you should come to Izmir tomorrow. Write down this address—you will stay in my condo. The doorman will let you in."

Art carefully penned the address. "Thank you. I really can't imagine being alone through all of this."

"Call me tonight once you know more."

"Will do, thanks for the good advice and your prayers. I really need them about now."

When Art hung up, he realized he hadn't eaten anything yet today but he wasn't hungry. Yet he knew that if he didn't keep a semblance of his normal routine he would not be able to function very well. So he decided to go to a little fish shack and have a simple lunch. They say in Turkey that fish is brain food, so maybe a fresh fish sandwich would help him think things through clearly.

As he was walking down the hill from the Sea Pines it dawned on Art just how much Marissa had come to mean to him. Things didn't seem at all normal without her around. There was a vacuum, a void. Art had already gotten used to sharing his life with Marissa, and now he felt lost, and completely at a loss to know what to do next. One of the strange things about life is that when you are in a personal crisis, you have a hard time understanding why no one around you seems to understand the gravity of the situation. The children at the elementary school on the boulevard were playing and having a big time, full of fun and laughter. Something inside of Art wanted to yell at them as he went past, "Don't you know you shouldn't be happy right now?" But of course they were oblivious to his plight. Life goes on, whatever may happen to a particular individual or family.

Art was contemplating this when he sat down at a seaside table and ordered the fried calamari instead of the sandwich. The seagulls were flying overhead and seemed to be mocking him with their screeches. Art thought, "You're like Job's comforters!"

The food came in about ten minutes—hot and tasty. Art washed it down with an Ephes beer, the local favorite. With nowhere to go and nothing to do, Art just stared out at the waves as they crested and then fell, and crested and fell. The waves were small in Kushadasi on this day, and Art allowed himself to daydream of the night he and Marissa had spent together two days ago. He had never known he could feel like that, feel so much a part of another person, so one with another person. His dark sunglasses hid the tears in his eyes as images of his wedding day swirled in his mind. Quietly he said, "Lord, would you please do something about this. I really can't handle it. It's too close to my heart, and my heart is breaking."

Just then he heard a familiar voice. "Art? Is that you?"

Art looked up and there standing in front of him was Meltem Ciftci. "What is wrong Art? Stand up and let me give you a hug!"

Art obliged and whispered in his friend's ear, "They have taken my wife away, and I don't know where they have put her."

A shocked look came over Mel's face. "What!! Are you saying Marissa has been kidnapped?"

"Yes Mel, by the Circle of Five, those terrorists who apparently killed two Christian priests. It happened this morning. Marissa went out to the beach and didn't come back. I have a note from the kidnapper in my pocket."

She read the note with eyes widening, and looked at Art with real fear. "We need to call Levent. He'll know what to do," she said quietly.

"I already have. I'm going to stay at the Sea Pines tonight and probably go to Izmir tomorrow. Levent has arranged for me to stay at his home."

"That's very good. I'm leading a tour group and we just checked into the Sea Pines as usual. They will be having lunch and exploring Kushadasi on their own for the rest of the day. There is a final dinner tonight at 8:00. Tomorrow I take them to Izmir for their return flight. So, for now, I will stay with you." She tried her best to comfort her longtime friend, but it was an uphill battle.

The day dragged on and on. Art and Mel wandered around town and eventually returned to the Sea Pines. Finally, the fateful hour rolled around.

Art said, "I have to call this number now and find out what's next. Will you stay with me?"

"Of course, of course. What are friends for anyway?" Taking out his cellphone and carefully punching in the numbers, Art heard the phone ring three times and then a gruff voice said, "Speak, infidel!"

"This is Art West and I was told to call this number and you would tell me what to do to get my wife back!"

There was a laugh at the other end. "Mr. West, your wife is in a lot of trouble, but perhaps something can be arranged. I am thinking she is priceless to you, so I am thinking you would move heaven and earth to get her back—yes??"

"Of course," said Art who was now clenching his teeth and getting very angry.

"Good! Then perhaps we can come to an understanding, but there must be no police, no funny business at all. Do you understand? Otherwise, your wife is dead and you will never see her again."

"Can I speak to my wife to be sure she is still alive at least."

"No, she is not here with me. I am, as you would say, the negotiator. She is not here. But at some point I can arrange that. For now, I assure you she is alive—although she might have a headache for a while!" He laughed again. "Here is what you must do next. You must acquire one million U.S. dollars and have it put into a banker's check. We will tell you where to deliver it on our next call. I will be calling you, not the other way around. You have 24 hours to make your arrangements. Then I will call again. Remember, your wife's life is on the line here. No nonsense, no police. Am I clear?"

"Crystal clear. What if I can't come up with that much money in just one day?"

"You don't want to know the answer to that question, so get it done," and then the phone went dead.

"What is the ransom?" asked Mel fearing the worst.

"One million U.S. dollars! Where in the world can I get that?" asked Art with a lost look on his face. Mel was quiet, and had no answer.

"I'm going to phone a friend, a banker in the U.S.—Dick Character. He has access to my archaeology funds. Maybe he can help."

And the call was made and the money began to flow through international channels. And Art prayed fervently that his plan would work. Tomorrow he would go to Izmir.

44

MARISSA'S ROUGH RIDE

MARISSA AWOKE IN THE trunk of a car while it was still moving. Her mouth was taped shut; her hands and feet were bound; and she was blindfolded. The smell of the exhaust was sufficient to make her choke from time to time. She was cramped and every joint ached.

Marissa vaguely remembered being attacked, but she didn't want to think about that. What she concentrated on was Art, and how frantic he must be. So she decided she would do her best to calm herself down and just pray for Art and her own situation. She had seen God do amazing things before, bringing Art back from death's door,[1] and God could resolve this situation as well. An unnatural calm prevailed in Marissa's heart, and she began thinking clearly. Where was she going? Wherever it was, it was in Turkey, a country she knew well. Somehow this journey was testing and strengthening her faith. Marissa firmly believed that.

It seemed like another hour of riding passed before the car abruptly stopped, then started again, then stopped, then started again a minute or so later. She must be in a town with stop lights. But where? Marissa could hear the traffic whizzing by outside, and it was an odd experience to travel lying down trying to visualize what she was hearing. Finally, the car came to a stop and did not start again. Marissa heard footsteps coming around to the back of the car which was parked in a quiet alley. The trunk swung open but immediately she was chloroformed and lost consciousness. Aziz glanced

---

1. This tale is told in the third Art West adventure, *Papias and the Mysterious Menorah*.

around—no one was watching. He swung Marissa onto his left shoulder, and carried her down the alley and into a small courtyard.

As he was heading into the back of the building, an old lady called out from her apartment window. "Is she okay? What is wrong?"

Aziz merely replied, "My sister is drunk!"

The old lady closed the shutters of her apartment and shook her head disapprovingly.

Aziz carried Marissa up two flights of stairs to the door of an apartment. He put her body down; found the key; unlocked the vacant apartment door; and dumped his prize on the couch in the far corner in the living room. Aziz was hot, exhausted, and cranky. Locking the door behind him, he flipped out his cellphone and called Iskender. "Mission accomplished. The bird is in the cage in Izmir. And believe me, you owe me!"

"Maybe so," said Iskender. "I hope no one saw you. I will be in touch with West today, and we will see how things go. Whatever you do, don't let that woman out of your sight. Understand? Just make sure she's tied up and blindfolded! Make sure she doesn't see you."

"I have to eat you know! And she's wearing a bathing suit and some little shorts—disgusting for a woman," complained Aziz.

"We will send over a woman to bring food and clothes—and a *keffiyeh* for you to wear. I don't want her to ever see you! Understood?" growled Iskender.

"Fine! Make it good food. And a *burka* would be good for her!" snapped Aziz.

"Use your phone to take a picture of her right now. It's all I've got to convince West his wife is still alive."

Aziz did as he was told. Now he was stuck babysitting Marissa for who knew how long. He didn't tell Iskender about the old woman in the window.

45

ABDULLAH'S DECISION

THINGS HAD BEGUN TO look grim for Abdullah. His home had been raided by Mosad before his family could finish packing. His wife sent a message that they would be detained indefinitely if he did not turn himself in. But if he did turn himself in, he could be tried as a terrorist and not merely as a thief, since the theft was done in order to support Hamas. And that meant a possible life in prison, and that was the lesser of two evils! What should he do? He decided he needed advice from the local Imam.

The walk from the safe house to the nearby mosque took only a matter of minutes, but the distance Abdullah was travelling in his thoughts was endless. Had he done the right thing for Allah in stealing the manuscript? But the manuscript was by a holy prophet that is revered in Islam, Issah [Jesus]! Was it a good thing he was helping Hamas, or not? He had mixed feelings, and above all he wanted his family to be left alone. Abdullah sat on a prayer rug in front of the Imam, an elderly man with a snow-white beard and moustache. He listened intently to Abdullah's tale of woe. Finally he asked a question.

"What made you think stealing something might be Allah's will for you?"

"Imam, I was told by members of Hamas that this would be seen as a good deed, even a noble deed, by Allah, blessed be He. Were they wrong?"

"Yes son, they were wrong, especially since the Koran is clear about stealing something that was never yours. Furthermore, you stole something about or by the holy man Issah, a prophet who is revered in the Koran. Imagine if you had been asked to steal something written by Mohammed in some museum in Mecca. You wouldn't even have listened to such a request."

Abdullah hung his head. "I thought I would be helping Hamas, and now I see I have ruined my family. But what should I do now? I don't want my family to suffer for my foolishness. If I give myself up, I will probably never see my family again." At this Abdullah broke down and wept.

The Imam was wise enough to let the man grieve, but after a few minutes he said firmly, "Allah will honor the sacrifice of good intent you make now, and everything will turn out *ensh'Allah* [as God wills]. My advice is to make the exchange and free your family, and then pray for mercy on your sins."

With this pronouncement, Abdullah simply nodded his head. He knew what he had to do. The deed was simple, but the repercussions profound. He would simply walk the mile or so to the checkpoint at the border, and turn himself over to the Israeli border guards. It would be hard to imagine a more dejected man than Abdullah Hashimi. The words of the Imam made him realize that his work for the radical Hamas had not been to the glory of Allah. For him, it had just been about revenge for wrongs done to Palestinians, including some of his own relatives.

Reluctantly, but with commitment, Abdullah trudged to the check point after calling Mosad and telling them he would give himself up in exchange for the release of his family. They readily agreed to this deal, since his family was guilty of no crime. He promised he would tell all about the theft of the manuscript once his family was free once more.

The Palestinian guards looked at Abdullah, and when he told them his intent, one of them said, "Don't do it! You will probably be in jail the rest of your life!"

Abdullah replied, "Better that than my whole family being under constant harassment by the Israelis. It's not their fault; it was my own choices that landed me in this spot."

And with that he asked that the gate be raised so he could cross over into Israeli territory where a jeep was waiting for him. Though the walk was only a few feet, each step was painful. And when he was handcuffed and placed in the back of the jeep next to one of the guards, Abdullah began to weep silently. He felt betrayed by his own people in Hamas and, oddly enough, he felt he had betrayed people who had been kind to him, especially Sammy Cohen and his Rabbi.

"The world is upside down when your friends betray you, and your enemies are good to you," he said to himself. Then he remembered a famous saying of the prophet Issah—"Love your enemies, and pray for those that persecute you." As he rode across the desert heading back to Jerusalem, he also remembered reading the translation of a couple of the beatitudes he had seen in the Jesus scroll. "Blessed are the poor in spirit, for theirs is the kingdom of heaven."

"It's funny," said Abdullah to himself as the jeep bumped along the desert dirt road. "The Imam said to me that violence was not the route to Paradise, but rather love, meekness, and kindness. The proud and arrogant in spirit will not enter Paradise, but the poor in spirit. That's what Issah said as well. I should have listened; I should have listened." Then Abdullah remembered a famous saying he was taught in school, a saying of the American poet John Greenleaf Whittier who ended his poem, *Maud Muller*, with these memorable words: "For of all sad words of tongue or pen, the saddest are these: 'It might have been.'"

46

ANCIENT SMYRNA/ MODERN IZMIR

ACCORDING TO REVELATION 2:8–11 the church in Smyrna was poor and persecuted.

> These are the words of him who is the First and the Last, who died and came to life again. 9 I know your afflictions and your poverty—yet you are rich! I know about the slander of those who say they are Jews and are not, but are a synagogue of Satan. 10 Do not be afraid of what you are about to suffer. I tell you, the devil will put some of you in prison to test you, and you will suffer persecution for ten days. Be faithful, even to the point of death, and I will give you life as your victor's crown. Whoever has ears, let them hear what the Spirit says to the churches. The one who is victorious will not be hurt at all by the second death.

By the early second century, Polycarp was Bishop of Smyrna (modern-day Izmir), and his friend Papias was the Bishop in nearly Hierapolis (modern-day Pamukkale). The church was growing, but still under persecution. Polycarp himself was eventually martyred.

Art knew there was a long, long history of Christian persecution here until the golden age of Constantine when all of Turkey was Christianized, albeit by decree. From the time of the Edict of Milan signed in 313, to the Fall of Constantinople at the hands of the Ottoman Turks in 1453, Christianity was the official religion.

Following the defeat of the Ottomans in World War I, Mustafa Kemal Atatürk became the first President of Turkey. His amazing reforms transformed the Ottoman Empire into a modern secular nation that allowed freedom of religion—to a point.

Patriarch Bartholomew dealt with the uneasy peace between the Christians and Muslims on a daily basis. He was still trying to get the government to reopen the Halki Seminary on Princes' Islands in the Sea of Marmara. The government found a way to close it in 1971, claiming that private schools were not allowed. Statesmen from all over the world had defended the Patriarch many times to no avail.

In 2009, President Barack Obama said in a speech in Turkey, "Freedom of religion and expression lead to a strong and vibrant civil society that only strengthens the state, which is why steps like reopening the Halki Seminary will send such an important signal inside Turkey and beyond. An enduring commitment to the rule of law is the only way to achieve the security that comes from justice for all people."

The Patriarch himself had been a target of extremists. So it was no great surprise when Art called him from Izmir and informed him that Marissa had been kidnapped by the Circle of Five—the same radicals now believed responsible for the deaths of two clerics, including his close friend Father Demetrios.

"My dear Doctor West, this news grieves me so. I feel led to tell you that you should stay in Izmir and tend to this dreadful matter. The business we have with the House of Mary can certainly wait! I am deeply moved that you would worry so about our plans to meet. Stay in Izmir but keep me informed as best you can. I keep many secrets, and I will treat your situation with the utmost of confidentiality. Blessings and prayers, my son!"

When Art hung up, he was crying. He resolved not to make any more phone calls. Right now, Art was sitting in the high-rise apartment of Levent Oral whose wife Natali was coaxing some lentil soup and crackers into Art.

"You must eat," she was insisting. "You are no good to Marissa if you are wasting away."

"I know, I know. But it's hard to eat when your insides are churning. I wish the boss of this group of radicals would go ahead and call."

As if on cue, Art's cellphone rang, and he was so anxious to take the call he dropped the cell phone on the floor as he was trying to flip it open. Finally he squeaked out, "Hello?"

Iskender loudly said, "Listen very carefully. Your wife's life may depend upon it. Tomorrow, at 9 A.M. you are to go to the National Bank on Ataturk Boulevard in Izmir. Here is the banking account number—043-911-942-8715M. You are to deposit the $1 million dollars into that account. Once I confirm that the money is where it should be, then I will give the orders to have your wife released unharmed at a location I will tell you tomorrow."

"Can you at least tell me what city she will be released in? And how do I know she's even alive?" asked an anxious Art.

There was a pause at the other end of the line as if Iskender was thinking. Finally he said abruptly, "She is in Izmir. And I am sending you a picture of your wife—unconscious—but definitely alive!"

The phone went dead and Art stared at his friends. "He claims she's in Izmir, so at least I'm in the right place. Right? It's interesting that the Patriarch told me not to leave Izmir. Strange!"

Then the picture of Marissa came through on the cell phone. They all gathered around and stared at the picture in stunned silence.

Art said, "She is alive—I can't even consider that I'm looking at Marissa's dead body. So, do you know where the National Bank on Atatürk Boulevard is? I don't. This is where I'm supposed to go in the morning and deposit the money. Of course, now I need to get the money from Barclays before the bank closes. My banker, Richard Character, promised it would be transferred today. Can I borrow your car?" said Art rambling almost incoherently at this point.

"I will drive you," said Levent smiling calmly. "Keep your spirits up and eat your soup!"

47

WAIT UNTIL DARK

MARISSA SLEPT MOST OF Thursday night on the couch thanks to the bump on the head and the dose of chloroform. Aziz nodded off occasionally as he sat in a large chair opposite the couch.

First thing in the morning, two women hired by Iskender brought food, clothes for Marissa, and an Arab head covering to disguise Aziz's face. Aziz was disappointed that they didn't bring a *burka*. He would rather have Marissa covered from head to foot, but such garb was now illegal in secular Turkey. "It's disgusting what those loose women wear these days in public," thought Aziz.

The smell of coffee actually aroused Marissa from her sleep. She moaned as she awoke. Aziz swigged down his coffee and grabbed his pistol. Considering she was still bound, gagged, and blindfolded, what did he have to fear from this vulnerable woman?

Marissa attempted to talk through the gag. This broke the tension for Aziz who actually laughed. "Just shut up! I'm going to remove your gag. I have a gun and if you make any screams then I will use it to knock you out again!" threatened Aziz. "If you understand, then nod your head."

When she complied, he took off the gag. Immediately, Marissa sputtered, "Take off this blindfold! It's giving me a headache. I'm hungry and I want a bathroom!"

Her feisty attitude took Aziz by surprise, but he knew he had the upper hand. "Blindfold stays. Headache will go away. Eat first. Then we consider bathroom."

"I want to use the toilet first!" she demanded.

"That is more of a problem. But I have orders to make sure you are worth the money being paid, so I will untie you and push you into the bathroom. You can take off the blindfold in there—and put it on when you are finished. Do you understand, you foolish woman?!"

"I'm smarter than you think," smiled Marissa who wisely decided not to rile him anymore.

After being unbound, Marissa's wrists and ankles ached, and she discovered she was a bit wobbly, but knowing Aziz had a gun pointing at her, she let him lead her to the bathroom.

"There's a bundle of clothes on the floor. I'm tired of looking at your body. You shame Allah. Put them on," he demanded.

Once inside, she happily pulled off the blindfold. Despite the stench in the dirty room she used the toilet. Then she turned on the sink faucet and drenched her face and hair with the cool water. Finally, she changed out of her bathing suit and running shorts. The clothes were a bit baggy but suitable. She even put on the traditional headscarf. Looking up she noted a window above the toilet so she climbed up on the toilet seat, and what did she see but an enormous stone image of President Ataturk not two hundred yards away on a hill across a busy highway!

Marissa could hardly believe it! She was actually in the town she knew very well—Izmir! And now she knew exactly where she was being held. She was a long way from home in Ankara and her flat in Istanbul, but the familiar sight of the first President of Turkey moved her deeply. She must think carefully about how to deal with her captor. Maybe she could learn more about his plans.

"Time to come out of the toilet unless you want me to come in and get you! And put your blindfold back on," snarled Aziz who was now wearing the keffiyeh, the traditional Arab head covering for men. "I hate this thing—I feel like a camel driver," complained Aziz to himself.

To Marissa he added in a menacing tone of voice, "I would love a reason to force you to do my bidding!"

Marissa obeyed and emerged in her new outfit. "I'm hungry now," she informed him calmly.

Aziz was both a fundamentalist fanatic and a male chauvinist. His prejudices he took for principles, and his principles he took for absolute truths. In the case of women, he was certain that they were not as intelligent or as brave as men. This belief led to an assumption that Marissa did not have it within her to risk her life trying to escape.

"So how long will I be here?" asked Marissa sweetly, as she sat on the couch trying to feed herself blindfolded.

"What? You don't like my company? Feeling is mutual. So the answer is, not long I hope. The ransom will be paid tomorrow, although I can't imagine why anyone would bother," sneered Aziz. For now, Marissa got the information she wanted.

The day was boring. Aziz was glued to the Turkish TV; Marissa could only listen. Hours dragged by. Lunch was brought at 2. Marissa was untied and retied. Toilet breaks were allowed. Marissa was untied and retied. Supper was brought at 8 followed by another toilet break. Marissa was untied. After using the toilet, she quietly opened the door and peaked out. Aziz had his back to her and his eyes glued to a soccer match on TV. Marissa slipped back to the couch, still untied, and put on her blindfold. Eventually Aziz glanced over but saw a demure woman sitting quietly with her hands behind her back and a blindfold on. "That's the way it should be with women," he thought.

When midnight rolled around, Aziz slid another couch across the apartment door. Iskender called to remind him to stay alert. He did for several hours late into the night. Finally, there were no more games to watch and Aziz dozed off, confident that Marissa couldn't possibly be a problem. His snoring grew deeper and louder.

Marissa, on the other hand was very much awake. She removed her blindfold and stared at Aziz without moving a muscle, fearing that he might wake up. But he snored deeply. And then she just knew—it was the man who offered her a cold drink—the Good Samaritan. She was sure.

Marissa was not on the ground floor and the door was blocked. Quietly, ever so quietly, Marissa walked into the bathroom and locked the door. She could still hear the snoring in the next room. Opening the window while standing on the toilet tank was easy enough, but pulling herself up to a level where she could get out took a lot of arm strength. Nevertheless, she decided to try it. It was very dark, and she had no idea what awaited on the other side of the window. Would she drop directly to the ground? How far down was it? Was it worth the risk?

A peace came over her as she began to pray. There was no sense of foreboding or fear—just a sense of calm. Standing on tiptoe she managed to grab a strong hold on the bottom of the window, and then she slithered out and onto a ledge. It was a cloudy night, no stars could be seen, and there were no lights in the courtyard below. Marissa could see very little, but she could smell freedom.

48

DON'T BANK ON IT

MORNING CAME, AND ART had on his night table the check from Barclay's. He had never seen a check for a million dollars before, but there it was made out for deposit to an obviously dummy business! The bank opened at nine and with a feeling of sadness, but firm resolve, Art was going to go do what had to be done.

There was no reason for them to let Marissa go, especially if she had seen any of them. He prayed they had been smart enough not to allow that to happen. But they could get the money and eliminate a target of their hatred if they wanted to. There was no reason to think they would keep faith with what they said. So a sense of dread came over Art. All in one morning he could lose his wife and a huge sum of gift money, money for further research and archaeological work.

"Please Lord," said Art to himself as he got out of bed. "Don't let it happen. I will gladly give up the money, but not my Marissa please. Not that. You just gave her to me. I can't lose her so soon."

Levent and Natali tried to get Art to eat breakfast. Instead he sat quietly on the balcony of their apartment, looking out over the city of Izmir. She was out there somewhere—lost amongst the 3 million people in the metropolitan area who made Izmir their home. After breakfast, Levent came out to the balcony and offered him the sports page telling all about the Fenerbahçe Sports Club's latest soccer signing.

Levent then said quietly, "Let's go for a ride, Art. The bank is only open from 9–12 on Saturday."

Kissing Natali goodbye, Levent headed out the door with Art right behind him. Now the nervous feeling in Art's stomach was beginning to get more and more insistent. Art was holding a manila folder concealing the check and record of the wire transfer.

In the passenger seat, Art sat and watched all the usual morning mayhem in a big city even though it was Saturday—the street cleaning machine, the kiosks selling coffee, customers lining up for coffee, bread venders pushing their carts, minions running errands, buskers entertaining tourists, panhandlers just hoping for a lira. Rows of palm trees lined the streets, but not a frond moved—the air was still and hot.

Reaching over Levent patted Art on the hand and said, "God is at your side to see you through anything."

Art managed a weak smile. Of course in his mind he knew and believed this to be true, but he also knew that in a fallen world, bad things happen to good people. Yes, God would be at his side no matter what the outcome. If he lost Marissa, God would be there to comfort him. If he found Marissa, God would be there to rejoice with him.

After another fifteen minutes of stop and go traffic, finally the First National Bank was sighted on Ataturk Boulevard. There were no signs of activity yet at the bank, but it was still ten minutes before opening time. Art sat waiting, but he did not see any lights coming on in the large lobby of the building, nor anyone inside. One man ran up the steps, stopped, peered inside, turned and left. Strange! Finally, not being able to wait any longer, Art got out of the car, walked up the steps, and noticed there was a piece of paper taped to the inside of the massive wrought-iron door. Calling to Levent he said, "There's a note here—I can't read it!"

After leaping out of the car and bounding up the stairs, Levent read the makeshift temporary sign, and then his countenance fell. Art looked frantically at Levent. "What does it say?"

"There's no explanation," replied Levent shaking his head and looking puzzled. "It just says, bank closed—reopening Monday—sorry for the inconvenience."

Levent managed to make Art sit down in the car, drink some water and calm down enough to think rationally. They decided to call Iskender immediately.

"So I'm going to explain that I have the check in hand, but the bank is closed until Monday. Right? In short, tell the truth, as improbable as it sounds."

"The truth is always the best. He can verify your story easily with a simple phone call to the bank," explained Levent. "Let's hope he wants his money bad enough to wait."

So Art called, and a gravelly voice was heard at the other end of the line. "Speak!"

"This is Arthur West. I'm at the bank just like you told me. The bank is closed. No explanation. Just a note on the door. It's not my fault! I have the check in my hand! The bank won't be open until Monday. I am not stalling! I wouldn't do anything to jeopardize Marissa's life. You can check it yourself!" said Art surprising himself with his forcefulness.

"Dammit," said the voice at the other end, and then he put his hand over the mouthpiece and yelled in Turkish to someone else in the room. "You had better not be lying to me."

"Trust me, I'm not! My wife is too important to me!"

"Good. You keep thinking that thought." Two minutes later, Iskender's computer geek came back to him with supporting news. "So it seems you are not lying."

"No! And I want to talk to my wife—you have to assure me that she is still alive."

"Tonight you will talk to your wife. And I guarantee she will say to you that you will deliver the money on Monday morning. For now, she stays with us," promised Iskender.

"No wife, no money," said Art feeling braver.

"No money, no wife," responded Iskender unshaken.

49

KAHLIL THE MYSTIC

KAHLIL EL SAID WAS a Sufi Muslim. No, he did not do the whirling dervish dance like Turkish Muslims of the Mevlevi order. But when he went into a deep prayer mode, he could be out there in the spiritual realm for quite a long time indeed. His daughter Hannah was a more down to earth sort of person, but she had learned to simply leave her father alone, and not interrupt in any way when he was communing with the divine.

On this Saturday morning, Kahlil had been deeply troubled in his spirit. It was one of those indefinable things that Kahlil could not explain to Hannah. Something was terribly wrong somewhere in the world of the people that Kahlil loved and prayed for regularly. Kahlil was taking his petition to the Almighty without knowing quite what to say.

Kahlil was one of those persons who had a strong sense of the divine presence from time to time, and usually it brought him to his knees. Kahlil felt led to pray for healing, but who it was that needed healing he had no idea. His own more distant relatives seemed fine; his friends in Jerusalem seemed fine; baby Samuel and Hannah were fine; Grace, Manny and Yelena were fine. Art and Marissa should be back in Istanbul after their honeymoon and surely must be fine. So, it was a puzzle, but not a puzzle he felt he needed to solve before praying.

Rolling out his prayer mat on the floor of the antiquities shop, he began reading Gibran's poetic words on prayer.

You pray in your distress and in your need; would that you might pray also in the fullness of your joy and in your days of abundance. For what is prayer but the expansion of yourself into the living ether?

And if it is for your comfort to pour your darkness into space, it is also for your delight to pour forth the dawning of your heart.

And if you cannot but weep when your soul summons you to prayer, she should spur you again and yet again, though weeping, until you shall come laughing.

When you pray you rise to meet in the air those who are praying at that very hour, and whom save in prayer you may not meet.

Therefore let your visit to that temple invisible be for naught but ecstasy and sweet communion.

For if you should enter the temple for no other purpose than asking you shall not receive:

And if you should enter into it to humble yourself you shall not be lifted:

Or even if you should enter into it to beg for the good of others you shall not be heard.

It is enough that you enter the temple invisible.

I cannot teach you how to pray in words. God listens not to your words save when He Himself utters them through your lips.

And I cannot teach you the prayer of the seas and the forests and the mountains.

But you who are born of the mountains and the forests and the seas can find their prayer in your heart,

And if you but listen in the stillness of the night you shall hear them saying in silence,

Our God, who art our winged self, it is thy will in us that willeth. It is thy desire in us that desireth.

It is thy urge in us that would turn our nights, which are thine, into days which are thine also.

We cannot ask thee for aught, for thou knowest our needs before they are born in us: Thou art our need; and in giving us more of thyself thou givest us all.

"Be still, and know that I am God," said Kahlil remembering a verse from the Bible. For the next hour, Kahlil prostrated himself on his prayer rug seeking to be free of his ego and to be one with Allah. He asked for help for someone amongst his circle of loved ones. When he finally arose from his prayer mat, Kahlil was stiff as a board. Getting up and down was not easy any more.

"Hannah, I feel a burden lifted spiritually, but lifting myself up is more difficult! I don't know what that was all about, but what I do know is that Allah is on the move, and he does nothing idly. He did not lay this burden on my heart to pray for nothing."

"I agree, so we will just have to abide our souls in patience, Father, and see what transpires."

"*Ensh'allah*, as God wills and in God's time."

50

RUN FOR YOUR LIFE!

MARISSA LANDED ON THE ground with a thud and a very loud yelp of pain. She rolled onto her side, clenched her teeth, and drew in several sharp breaths. Another loud cry uncontrollably escaped her. Tears welled up in her eyes. The twenty-foot drop from the window sprained her right ankle upon landing. However painful, she needed to get away.

The first yelp was enough to arouse Aziz from his sleep; the second snapped him to attention. He turned on a light only to discover that his prize was not on the couch. He went into the bathroom—Marissa was not there. He looked up—the window was wide open! Then he ran down the two flights of stairs, gun in hand. He looked about the courtyard—no Marissa. There was only one way out—up the alley where he had parked the car. From there it was a maze of narrow streets.

Hobbling, Marissa made it up the alley which led to a street that led to the main road. Keeping sight of the brightly lit rock face of Ataturk, Marissa made her way towards the highway. Stepping off the curb, she frantically waved her hands at a car approaching from some ways off.

By now Aziz was closing in—he spotted her up ahead near the highway. And Marissa saw a man running toward her—it must be Aziz. She began to panic, the sweat pouring down her face.

The driver had three choices—go around her, hit her, or stop! But Marissa was yelling, "Please, help!" In a split second he made his decision and slammed on the brakes.

Seeing a man coming full speed straight toward Marissa, he turned his body, opened the back door of his car, and yelled to Marissa, "Jump in—NOW!" Adrenalin propelled Marissa to dive into the back seat. At that same moment, two shots rang out—one shattered the back window and one passed through her arm and entered her back. The driver slammed his foot on the gas, and the jolt slammed the back door shut.

Bleeding profusely, Marissa managed to say, "I've been hit! I'm Marissa Okur. I was kidnapped!" And then there was pain so severe that she blacked out.

By a singular providence of God, the driver was a well-known pediatrician, Malik Polat, on his way to prepare for early morning rounds. The Ege University Hospital is one of Izmir's best, and its trauma center unparalleled. Malik knew it was her best chance.

Using his car phone, he called the police. "This is Doctor Malik Polat—I've got a woman in my car with a GSW. Says she was kidnapped. Meet me at University Hospital. And look for a man with a gun around the apartments across from the Ataturk monument!"

Aziz lingered briefly on the side of the highway, trying to deal with the fact that Marissa was gone and perhaps even dead. He slowly walked back to the flat, wondering how he would tell Iskender he had lost Marissa West. Halfway back, he sat on the curb and began to call Iskender. An alert patrol car spotted Aziz and turned on his siren. Aziz dropped the phone. After a short chase, he found himself being handcuffed, too winded and too downcast to even resist.

51

SAVING MARISSA

THE EMERGENCY TEAM WHEELED a gurney out to the car and carefully transferred the limp, bleeding woman. The head nurse notified Malik that the police wanted to talk to him about a kidnapped woman.

Sitting in the lobby with Detective Rahmi Asker, Malik related everything he could remember and Marissa's exact words: "I'm Marissa Okur. I was kidnapped."

"We have no record of any recent kidnappings in Izmir," replied the detective, pad in hand. "There are a lot of Okurs in this town, but this woman said her name was Marissa Okur, so we will start to track her down. She came in with no IDs. Do you think she'll pull through, Doc?"

"I don't know! I just drove straight to the hospital. I should've stopped! Done something! Now I understand better how people react in a crisis—and I do mean react. You don't think; you just react. But I'm going to follow this case—my morning rounds can wait awhile! I should call my wife," said the doctor suddenly realizing he was also in a state of shock.

"And your insurance people," added the detective. "I've got to impound your car for the investigation. What you did was very brave. You could be on that gurney, you know! Call that wife, Doc. Meanwhile, I'm calling headquarters."

The police eventually tracked down one Marissa Okur, archaeologist, whose family lived in Ankara. No one answered her cell phone. Headquarters sent him a photo which matched the victim."

"Thanks, said Detective Asker. I'll follow through with the family from here at the hospital." He dialed the Ankara number.

"*Efendim*? Who is calling please," asked Marissa's father, Zafer.

"This is Detective Asker in Izmir. Do you have a daughter named Marissa Okur?"

"Yes, of course, but she was recently married. She is now Marissa Okur West. In fact she is on her honeymoon with her husband."

"Mr. Okur. I have every reason to believe that your daughter Marissa is in University Hospital in Izmir. Apparently, she has been shot and is now in surgery. I can't tell you more about her condition yet. What is her husband's name and how can we get in touch with him?" By now, Zeliha, Marissa's mother, was standing by the phone, knowing that something must be terribly wrong.

"He is Arthur West—Dr. Arthur West. Like our Marissa, an archaeologist. They were married two weeks ago in Istanbul. I thought they had returned there by now, but I must admit I haven't heard from Marissa in a few days. My wife will give you his phone number," said Zafer.

"We will contact him. If possible, you may want to come here to Izmir," advised the Detective. After Zeliha spoke with the detective, Zafer immediately made plans to fly to Izmir.

~

Despite the fact that it was Saturday, Levent was stuck in some traffic as he drove back to the apartment with Art deep in thought beside him. Suddenly, Art's phone rang out causing them both to jump.

When Art picked up the phone the last thing he expected to hear was that his wife was fighting for her life in an Izmir Hospital! It took him a minute to actually grasp what Detective Asker was saying. He listened carefully all the while exchanging glances with Levent whose brow was becoming deeply furrowed.

"Levent, I have good news, and bad news," said Art almost in a whisper.

"Tell me the good news first."

"Marissa has been found!"

"Excellent! Now about the bad news."

"She is fighting for her life at University Hospital!"

Now it was normally calm, cool, and collected Levent who exclaimed, "What!"

"It's true, and we need to get over there as quickly as possible."

The trip to the hospital also was impeded by traffic, and the hospital parking lot was packed with cars, but Levent managed to squeeze into a small space. Art hit the ground running for the entrance to the emergency room, with Levent right behind him.

Once inside, Art stopped short, seemingly overwhelmed by all the activity. It was Levent who went to the desk and explained the situation. Immediately, they were both ushered into a small room where Detective Asker had a computer set up.

After introductions, Art asked for an update.

The Detective calmly obliged. "The bullet lodged in your wife's left kidney. The last update I got indicated that the kidney will be removed. A vein was severed in her arm resulting in loss of a lot of blood. There's also a wound on her head."

"How did she end up here?" asked Levent

"She was fortunate there. She was picked up on the side of the road by one of our local pediatricians, Malik Polat, who was on his way to early morning rounds. He brought her here at no small risk to his own life. Two shots were fired—one hit the car and the other hit your wife."

"How long will Marissa be in surgery?"

"Hard to tell. We are waiting for the surgeons report. I forgot to add that she also has a fractured ankle, probably from a fall."

Turning to Levent, Art looked as pale as a ghost. "She must have tried to escape, and somehow pulled it off, getting shot in the process."

"That brings me to another matter, Dr. West. You knew your wife was kidnapped?"

"Yes sir," replied Art slowly.

"And you never contacted the police."

"No sir," replied Art, again slowly. "They threatened to kill her if I didn't pay the ransom."

The Detective sighed deeply. "They all say that, Dr. West. And it usually ends badly. There's no reason for them to release their victim once they get their money. Have you paid the ransom?"

"I tried—but the answer is No!" And then Art explained what happened at the bank that morning.

Amazed, the Detective replied, "Someone is looking out for you, Dr. West! But let the professionals take over from here. You say you have the phone number of your contact and even a picture of your wife?" Just then the Detective's phone rang. After listening to the message, he replied with some irritation, "How come it took you so long to tell me this?" He hung up and turned to Art and Levent.

"Well, now we have the number of your contact, and we have the guy who shot your wife—apparently not the same person. He's spilling his guts downtown as we speak! You should stay here at the hospital for now, but I will need a full report eventually. I'm heading back to the station to interview the kidnapper. I will stay in touch." And with that the Detective handed Art his phone number, shook his hand, and left.

Levent put his hand on Art's shoulder. "Is there anyone you want to call? Her parents have been notified and I called Mel. She's finishing her tour today."

"I'm not ready to call people. I need to know more. I need to be more in control!" complained Art.

"Ah, said Levent, "That may not happen for a while! God is in control, remember? We must pray my friend. Right now, right here."

What came out of Art's mouth was the equivalent of a psalm of lament. "Oh Lord, I feel so helpless. I ask you to be Lord of the situation. I ask that you spare the life of my new wife. I ask you Jesus to be her personal healer. In your name I pray, Amen."

"Amen," echoed Levent.

52

JESUS ON DISPLAY

THE ENTRANCE ROOM BECKONED with well-lit exhibits on all four walls, including a display of Codex Alexandrinus, a fifth century manuscript of the Greek Bible, on loan from the British Library. But Pierre Saint-Saens knew it paled in comparison to the Jesus scroll, which was now sheltered in an oval room off the main exhibit. The tickets were not cheap, and the exhibit would run well into August, ensuring a tidy income for the Louvre this summer. After that, the Jesus scroll would become part of their permanent collection of ancient documents.

Pierre could hardly have been more thrilled at the advanced ticket sales—one million dollars already. Many of the days were already booked. Tour directors were calling in the hopes of getting special treatment.

On this opening night, champagne was flowing and only VIPs would gaze upon the document. The President would be there—bragging to his political friends that he was one of the first to see the manuscript. Ambassadors were eager to learn as much as possible about the scroll in order to entice their own political leaders to come to Paris. Media celebrities, fresh from their week at the Cannes film festival were in a party mood. Distinguished members of the Sorbonne and other universities were trying to sound knowledgeable as they discussed the find with one another. The über-wealthy of Paris (like the former über-wealthy of Ephesus) wore their jewels prominently. The elite press was awash in interviews. The paparazzi would have to wait outside the building.

Those that make Paris their home were begging for tickets. The jet setters would have to wait until later. There probably wouldn't be time enough this summer to accommodate everyone who genuinely wanted to see the exhibit.

Never mind that less than 1% of the viewers could read Aramaic. The first-century manuscript acted like a magnet drawing people to it. France, like other European countries, was a Jesus-haunted culture but biblically illiterate. Jesus was still a remarkable draw, even for the non-religious, and even for members of other faiths, like the growing population of Muslims in France.

Security was tight not only because of the value of the documents in the exhibit but also because of the stature of the guests invited to the glittery pre-showing. No one was to be allowed into the exhibit without giving up all personal items—handbags, cameras, cell phones, etc. No exceptions—not even for the President and his wife. Saint-Saens was taking no chances even if he ruffled some pompous feathers.

And when the *hoi polloi* were allowed in when the exhibit officially opened to the public, security would be even tighter. Single-file lines would be encouraged to move along by pushy guards. Traffic through the exhibit would be one-way and carefully controlled.

As Pierre stood in the midst of the gala nodding at influential people, he was insufferably pleased with himself. All was right with the world until Henri L'Matin showed up fuming and fussing. Grabbing his elbow, Henri firmly escorted Pierre to the far wall and said, "I was told that you tried to insinuate that the dealer, namely me, might have been a bit shady! Any more snide remarks like that, which directly or indirectly implicate me, and I will set my attack lawyers on you. You will go through legal misery for the foreseeable future, especially if the police start sniffing around my business practices. Get the picture?"

Saint-Saens pulled at his shirt collar. A vigilant guard started to walk their way, but Pierre waved him off. Regardless, he was shaken by the vehemence of Henri's words.

"Yes, Monsieur L'Matin, you may be sure I will say nothing to tarnish your name—I promised you anonymity after all. I apologize for the perceived slight," he said wondering to himself what he had done to deserve this insulting barrage.

"That's better, but heed my warning, no more pointing fingers in my direction or I'll be doing more than giving you the finger. I will be fingering you for dirty dealing."

"That will not be necessary. You can count on my silence."

"Good. And good luck with your exhibit. I hear the Israelis are clamoring for their precious scroll back," said L'Matin with a sarcastic smile on his face. "You'd better get ready to do battle." And with that he was gone.

To calm himself down, Pierre walked from the reception room down to the exhibit rooms. Saint-Saens could hear in his mind the money dropping into his coffers, and he smiled. Money might not buy you love, but it can calm your nerves sometimes.

53

FAMILY REUNION

WAITING IN ANTICIPATION IS when a child yearns for Christmas morning to arrive. Waiting in dread is when you fear things will turn out badly. Art was closer to the latter than the former. Late in the afternoon, when the first doctor emerged from surgery he did not look happy or hopeful.

The doctor's English was not the best, but Levent was present to help with the interpretation. After listening very carefully to the doctor's analysis, Levent paraphrased the verdict quite calmly and simply.

"The bottom line is that Marissa has come successfully through surgery, but she lost a kidney in the process. But there was also trauma to the spleen, which hopefully won't lead to more surgery. Marissa can also live without her spleen. The CT scan on her brain showed some venous blood clots as a result of the blow to her head, but they think that should clear up on its own with blood thinners. She could have some temporary stroke-like symptoms. And they put a cast on her fractured ankle. That about sums it up!"

"Can I see her?" pleaded Art. The doctor understood immediately and ushered Art into the recovery room. There lay Marissa—unconscious—buried under a blanket—surrounded by machines—tended by nurses and technicians. He touched her hand and turned away. The doctor escorted him out, fearing he would pass out. Art sat down shaking, and Levent provided a large glass of water. The doctor left but not without promising regular updates.

Minutes later, Marissa's near frantic parents showed up after their hour flight from Ankara. Art sat with them as Levent patiently repeated the same medical report. Fifteen minutes later, Meltem showed up in the waiting room after seeing her Tutku tour group off at the airport in the morning and spending time at her Izmir apartment. Mel and Levent had a quick meeting to catch up on business, and then she went to Art.

"How are you doing, my friend. I think you have been praying," she said. "God cares about what happens to Marissa. And he cares about you. When have you last eaten anything?" Mel and Levent then steered their little group to the cafeteria for some much-needed food.

Two hours came and went with the group now back in the waiting room. Levent headed home and Mel agreed to continue her vigil for the rest of the evening. The doctor reappeared to tell Art that things had not improved, but the vital signs were stable.

Mel whispered gently to Art, "Arthur, I have an idea, based on what you once lectured on in Ephesus. You were talking about miracles and magic, and the difference between the two. Jesus can do miracles when medical attention falls short—is that not your belief?"

"Yes. In fact, I've been thinking about that a lot lately."

"I have a friend here in Izmir. He is an American and he sometimes leads tours with us. He has lived here in Izmir for many, many years. He is what you call a Pentecostal, and even a faith healer. You may remember me speaking of him. His name is Mark Wilson. How do you feel about him coming and, as they say, placing his hands on Marissa? Isn't that some sort of anointing?"

"Oh yes, the laying on of hands goes back to the Old Testament and confers a blessing on the recipient. And in Acts 8, laying on of hands brings the Holy Spirit. And nowadays it's practiced regularly in faith healing services. But I'm rambling! This is no time for a lecture! Please call Mark. I'm eager to meet him!"

Suddenly, the doctor entered the waiting room once again, and all eyes turned to him, "Marissa's blood pressure is dropping which probably indicates more internal bleeding. We may need to do more surgery tonight!"

"That settles it," said Art with conviction. "Call Mark! But I don't know how Marissa's parents will react, to say nothing about the doctor!"

Mel said, "You are the husband. You deal with the in-laws. But let me deal with the good doctor! I can be very persuasive after all these years as a tour guide!"

54

AZIZ GRILLED

WHEN AZIZ WAS SEIZED by the police and dragged before the authorities in Izmir, the police had already been looking for the Circle of Five for some time. From his office in Istanbul, Detective Sadi Oguz had been tracking the killers of the two Christian priests. And increasingly, the finger pointed to Iskender and his gang who hung out near the Galata Tower. The names of all five had been determined. Four members in the gang had been trailed for over a week now. Tracing some of Iskender's phone calls had led Oguz to believe that Aziz was in Izmir. And it wasn't long before Oguz was told that Aziz had been arrested early Saturday morning on kidnapping charges. He was being held in the Izmir jail. It's a short flight to Izmir.

Late Saturday afternoon, Sadi himself was sitting in an interrogation room with an uncooperative Aziz who periodically spouted out fundamentalist rhetoric. Sadi's Izmir counterpart, Detective Rahmi Asker, fresh from the hospital, was calmly watching from the other side of the one-way mirror. A strong case was building against Aziz and his Circle of Five.

"So you will not talk to us, but no matter. We will let your cellphone do the talking for you. Do you recognize this woman?" Sadi showed Aziz the photo of Marissa bound and blindfolded." No response from Aziz.

"Well, let's listen to the very last message that you got from your leader, Iskender. He's in Istanbul, I believe, while you're stuck here in Izmir dealing with us," said Sadi rather sarcastically.

Aziz, listen! West is not going to deliver the money today because the bank is closed! You idiot! Why didn't you check? Keep that woman safe, you hear me! It's going down on Monday now. And why aren't you answering your phone, you fool!

"Let me guess! You didn't answer the phone because you were already in jail! Won't Iskender be surprised?!"

"He's the fool!" blurted out Aziz. "He should've known about the bank being closed. I was only supposed to . . ." and he stopped short.

"You were going to say that you were supposed to be guarding Marissa Okur—or I should say Marissa West, wife of Dr. Arthur West. You are part of the Circle of Five, but obviously not the brains. That would be Iskender, and I'm not so sure about him. Well, you will all have a nice reunion in Soganlik Prison in Istanbul with your fellow extremists."

Aziz simply spat on the floor. Finally he raised his head and said, "You are a disgrace to Allah, and he will deal with you in his time."

"Yeah, yeah. Did it occur to you that Allah might be dealing with you for your crimes right now, since Allah is not a fan of kidnapping and torturing Turkish women?"

"You are worse than the infidels! You do not even know the god of the Koran!" shouted Aziz, straining against the shackles which had his hands bound behind his back and chained to a metal chair.

"Well, we'll see whose version of justice is more righteous and approved by Allah soon enough. We are remanding you over to Justice Minister Sadullah Ergin and Istanbul's Police Chief Koksal. If your goal was to draw the attention of the authorities, you have succeeded very well indeed. Unlike the so-called justice you were handing out, we will at least give you a fair trial before imprisonment or execution. Your victims had no such justice."

With this, the Detective said, "You make me sick! You are the worst sort of Turk I can imagine. Get this man out of my sight, and send him to Istanbul!"

55

THE HEALING HANKY

MARK WILSON WAS A man on a mission. Mel's call brought him directly to the hospital. It took a good bit of persuasion, but Mel convinced the surgeon to allow the "holy man" and Art into the ICU. Only a few minutes would be allowed because preparations were already underway for repeat surgery.

Marissa's parents declined, preferring not to be involved with this Christian religious ceremony. It was going to take them some time to come to grips with the idea that their daughter was no longer a professing Muslim.

When Mark arrived, he was very business-like, since he didn't want to appear like some fanatic. Finally, he and Art were ushered into Marissa's room. At her bedside he found an almost unrecognizable woman hooked up to multiple monitors, her vital signs dipping dangerously.

Mark got out his anointing oil and made the sign of the cross on Marissa's forehead. Quietly, but loud enough for the nearby nurses to hear his words of petition, he prayed for immediate healing in the name of Jesus. But then he did something else that surprised even Art. He took out a handkerchief, prayed over it, anointed the cloth with oil from an olive tree growing in Ephesus, and laid the cloth across Marissa's forehead. With this he got down on his knees on the cold hard floor of the hospital room. Art joined him. Mark put one hand on Art's shoulder and with the other he held Marissa's hand. The two men bowed their heads in unison. Mark began praying first in English. He begged God to dramatically reverse what was happening to Marissa. He prayed for the healing of her organs, for the healing of her blood vessels, for the healing of her ankle. He prayed boldly for all of this to happen right now. Then he prayed quietly in tongues for a minute. It seemed as if time stood still for Art but in reality all of this occurred in the matter of five minutes.

The doctor stepped forward and got Art's attention. "We need you to leave now." Mark rose, leaned over Marissa, removed the hanky, and made the sign of the cross on her forehead one last time. Then he and Art left together.

This emotional venture had been draining, and when Mark went and sat down on the couch next to Art, he knew he had found a kindred soul and new friend. He had no qualms about telling Art how he felt during the healing ceremony.

"When I began praising God in tongues, my fingers started tingling. I felt power go out through my fingers and into her hand. Then my fingers went cold and stopped tingling. Now it's in the Lord's hands."

"But tell me, where did that handkerchief come from?" asked Art earnestly.

"Seriously, I bought it in the market at the entrance way to Ephesus. An elderly woman was selling them—each lovingly hand-made. I talked to her for some time. There was just something about her that seemed special to me."

"Are you telling me this was a healing hankie from Ephesus? Did she monogram Paul's initials on it?" actually laughing for the first time in days.

"I wish. But I always wanted to re-enact that story in Acts 19.11–12. It says that God worked unusual miracles through Paul. Even Paul's handkerchiefs or aprons or sweat bands or whatever could be laid on a person and that person would be healed. I don't normally do such a thing, but this hospital call was an unusual case for sure."

"I've been studying Ephesian magic and Ephesian miracles. I'm praying that Marissa's recovery will be an Ephesian miracle."

Mark smiled and noted, "God is in charge, no matter how we go about asking for his help."

"Amen to that!"

Quietly, Marissa's parents, Art, Mark and Mel waited and waited for 30 minutes. Finally the doctor emerged, strolled over to the group, put his hands in his pockets, and surveyed them with a bit of a quizzical look on his face before he spoke.

"Marissa's vital signs are improving steadily. Her blood pressure started rising back to nearly normal after you left. Her breathing is relaxed. Her good kidney seems to be functioning. Her hand twitched and there's some movement in her eyes. That could mean she's waking up slowly. I'm still going to do another CT scan on her abdomen and brain to determine the extent of bleeding, if there is any bleeding. For the moment, however, I'm holding off on further surgery. I've never witnessed a Christian healing ritual in my ICU. Maybe your God has answered your prayers!" With this he headed back to the ICU.

The group just sat there staring at each other. Marissa's parents were a bit dumbfounded. Mel gave Art yet another hug. Mark simply said, "Praise the Lord!" Then he left for home but not before promising Art that he would take him to some very interesting, off the beaten path, sites around Turkey in the future. "I lead a small house church here in Izmir. Whenever you and Marissa are in town again—and you will be—please visit my wife and I. You've got friends here."

Art checked his watch. "What time is it back in the States?" Art asked no one in particular. "I think it's time to spread some good news." Art began to make some phone calls beginning with his mother.

"This is a pleasant surprise! Are you back in Istanbul? I haven't talked to you in over a week. Did you call that nice Patriarch like I told you? He seemed so special. And let me tell you about my time with James Howell— I've been so worried lately. I just don't know why but he said I should pray more and . . ."

Art had to interrupt at this point. "Slow down Mom—and sit down if you aren't already. I have something important to tell you!" Then he related all the events of the past three days—Marissa's kidnapping in Kushadasi, his frantic efforts to pay the ransom money, and Marissa's escape in Izmir. Finally he told her about Mark Wilson who anointed Marissa with oil, laid hands upon her, and placed a healing hanky on her forehead.

"Right now, I can only tell you that she seems to be getting better and better. So the point is, start praying and don't stop. I just know God is working powerfully right now!"

Despite the long report, Joyce responded with a barrage of questions which Art tried to patiently answer. "Just call in the prayer warriors and please notify James and Jake and Melody!"

"Yes, I can be a warrior, not a worrier," promised his Mother.

Next, Art decided to call Kahlil, his best man. After telling his tale, Kahlil responded, "Ah, now I know why Allah spoke to me this morning. My day has been troubled knowing that someone needed the help of the Almighty. Thank you for calling. If it will help, I will contact your friends Grace and the others."

When Art hung up, the lyrics of Carole King's "You've Got a Friend," popped into his hand and he began to hum.

> Winter, spring, summer or fall; All you have to do is call; And I'll be there; You've got a friend.

56

THE HAND OF GOD

THE WEEK HAD GONE well for Monsieur Pierre Saint-Saens, and the cash register continued to ring. On Friday afternoon the curator was looking out the pyramidal glass entryway designed by I.M. Pei and watching a whopper of a thunderstorm over Paris. The city was not noted for its summer thunderstorms, but it had been extremely humid of late. People began to gather at the door marveling at the blackness of the clouds now racing across the sky in the direction of the Louvre.

Suddenly, huge bolts of lightning streaked down into the city. One of them struck the bank of transformers directly behind the Louvre, causing an unprecedented power surge, tripping every fuse in the museum. Lights flickered and went out. Fire broke out in the walls of two different sections of the museum, the two oldest sections that had the most antiquated electrical wiring. Smoke began to pour into rooms through the vents. Sprinkler systems inevitably kicked in. Backup generators provided eerie lighting.

The security guards were busy herding people down the ramp to the basement cafeteria for safety. Pierre was only worried about the manuscripts. Running from gallery to gallery he sought the source of the smoke. When he finally rounded the corner into the room housing the Jesus scroll, he stopped in horror when he saw smoke billowing from the vents and water spraying from the ceiling jets.

Panicking he took the butt end of a nearby fire extinguisher and smashed the glass case where the scroll lay. Ever so carefully he extracted the Jesus scroll from amongst the shards. Codex Alexandrinus, on loan to the Louvre, was next. Both of them got a little wet before he could cover them with his jacket and run out the door.

The French have a phrase to explain catastrophes—*main de Dieu*—the hand of God, not unlike the American phrase, 'an act of God.' Sometimes insurance companies do rightly recognize divine intervention when it happens. Pierre, to his horror, imagined the headlines in tomorrow's edition of *Le Monde—Le main de Dieu frappe du Louvre*—The hand of God strikes the Louvre.

On Saturday morning, the newspaper did indeed run an article hinting that the Hand of God had struck the Louvre. Director Jean-Luc Lambert was not pleased. A meeting of all the top curators who oversaw the Louvre's collections and staff of 2000 was set up for 9 AM sharp. Pierre Saint-Saens was put on the hot seat.

"What were you thinking? The scrolls were safe in their glass containers! Now they are bent and slightly water damaged!" cried the Director embarrassing Pierre nearly to tears.

The chief of security came to his defense. "It is possible that the sprinkler system would not have put out the flames. The ceiling could have caved in—we really don't know what could have happened to the scrolls. Slightly damaged scrolls are better than no scrolls!"

After the meeting, Pierre got up the courage to approach the Director and ask for a private meeting. "In my office in thirty minutes," scowled the Director.

Sitting down in a very comfortable green leather chair across from the desk of Director Lambert, Pierre launched into his plea. "As you know, our Jesus Scroll exhibit was bringing in record revenues to pay back the cost of the scroll itself, not to mention the cost to put on the exhibit. I did believe I was rescuing those scrolls! In any case, do you not think we should make it a top priority to reopen the exhibit as soon as possible—maybe even next week?" said Pierre hopefully.

Wrinkling his already very creased brow, the white haired gentleman across the desk squinted at Pierre and said, "Your request makes some financial sense. The insurance should cover our losses. I don't put any stock in those tabloids that are saying God struck the Louvre. The best I can do is put in a recommendation to the Ministry of Culture on Monday. But before I do that, what's this I hear about it being a stolen manuscript?"

Pierre cringed when this question was asked. In a timid voice, he replied, "I have heard that report as well, but the seller here in Paris assured me that he bought the document legally here in Paris from an antiquities dealer from Jerusalem. How that dealer got the manuscript, I honestly do not know. The trail is cold. I have been thinking however, that we should arrange some magnanimous favor for the Israeli Museum. How about an exhibit of some of our best Impressionist paintings perhaps? Just an idea. I do think we must keep hold of this precious Jesus scroll."

"We will do something to stop the Israeli authorities from barking at us, and I will recommend that we make the exhibit a priority. Is that satisfactory to you?"

With relief written all over his face Pierre replied, "I couldn't ask for more!" His day had taken a tremendous turn for the better. After striding out of the director's suite, he picked up speed and ran for his own small office to start planning the new and improved exhibit. However, he promised himself he would never do business again with Henri L'Matin. As he looked out the window from his office, he saw the sun breaking through the clouds with a single, slender column of light, shining directly on the Louvre.

"Maybe God is giving me a second chance," Pierre muttered to himself.

57

GRAYSON RIGHT ON Q

DESPITE THE RECENT JOURNEY of the Q scroll, Grace convened a preliminary study session with a mix of scholars, old and young, who were available on short notice. Many of the more famous were able to drop what they were doing and scramble to Jerusalem. The Q document was worth it.

One of the youngest scholars was Grayson Johnson who agreed to be the keynote speaker on the very first day of the symposium. Grayson was his own worst enemy, constantly under-rating himself even though he had published a few important articles on his work at Caesarea Philippi. Of course, his hippie demeanor often guaranteed that no one would take him seriously.

Today promised to be scorching on top of the Mount of Olives where Hebrew University sat. The visiting scholars were grateful to file into a comfortable air-conditioned room. Some, not all, of the old timers were enjoying meeting the up and comers and offering their sage advice. Some, not all, of the new kids on the block were in awe of the big name scholars. Certainly Grayson was despite having been mentored all these years by both Art West and Grace Levine.

Grayson finished his dissertation in record time under Grace's guiding hand. She was a no-nonsense advisor who didn't believe in prolonging the process. Timely feedback was her hallmark. Grayson walked the stage just a week ago and was already preparing to publish his dissertation on the importance of social and oral contexts for understanding the Gospel traditions. Today was his first public lecture behind a podium, and he was thinking he would rather be out on a dig!

Grace called all the scholars to order on this, the first day of the symposium. "Welcome to everyone who has traveled from near and far to join us here at Hebrew University. I trust you are eager to explore the Q scroll. Our first speaker is Dr. Grayson Johnson who will talk to you, appropriately enough, about the world of oral tradition!"

Grace had managed to get Grayson out of his signature tie-dyed t-shirts and into a gray suit with a bright yellow tie. His long hair was pulled back into a neat ponytail. Looking out in the audience, he glimpsed both Kahlil and Hannah who gave him the thumbs up. Grayson smiled and waved back, feeling ever more confident. His opening, "I'm glad you dudes all came" comment brought laughter from the crowd.

"Until now, the very existence of the Q document was hypothetical. And now, the study of the Q document is bedeviled by old assumptions about the nature of ancient texts and the transmission of such ancient texts. I suggest that we can't just rely on the old ways of doing things. What would happen if we took a genuinely fresh approach to this subject? Suppose we give more than lip service to the fact that this document was produced in a largely oral culture, and suppose we admit that this text, like almost all others in that age, is an oral text, a document meant to be heard rather than read? How might that change the landscape of our study? I'm proposing an oral context for studying the Q document.

"Ours is a text-based culture, a culture of written documents. The Internet age requires widespread literacy, which in turn leads to widespread production and reading of texts. It's difficult for us in a text-based culture to understand the character of an oral culture, much less understand how sacred texts function in such an oral culture.

"The literacy rate in biblical cultures was maybe five to twenty per cent depending on the culture and even the sub-group within the culture. Books were scarce. Papyrus was expensive, ink was expensive, and scribes were ultra-expensive. Ancient people, whether literate or not, preferred the living word, which is to say the spoken word. No wonder Jesus said to his audiences, 'Let those who have ears, listen' and not 'Let those who have eyes, read.' Most eyes could not read in the biblical period.

"I believe most documents in antiquity were meant to be read out loud usually to a group of people. This was particularly true of ancient letters, but also true of treatises and tracts. I would suggest that the Q document is just such an oral document. The sayings of Jesus were meant to be heard in the original language so that none of the oral effect of the words, none of the alliteration, assonance, rhythm, rhyme and pure poetry of Jesus would be lost in the process.

"In fact, most ancient documents including letters were not really texts in the modern sense at all. They were composed with their aural and oral potential in mind, and they were meant to be orally delivered when they arrived at their destination. Thus for example, when one reads the opening verses of Ephesians, loaded as it is with aural devices (assonance, alliteration, rhythm, rhyme, various rhetorical devices) it becomes perfectly clear that no one was ever meant to hear this in any language but Greek and furthermore, no one was ever meant to read this silently. It needed to be heard.

"As a cost saving measure, remember that a letter in Greek would have no separation of words or sentences, and little or no punctuation. It's just a string of capital letters—one after the other. The only way to decipher such a string of letters was to sound them out—out loud.

"Do you remember the famous anecdote about St. Augustine and St. Ambrose? Augustine said that Ambrose was the most remarkable man he had ever met, because he could read without moving his lips or making a sound. Clearly, an oral culture is a different world than our text-based culture. All sorts of texts were simply substitutes for oral speech. Once we realize that we are dealing in the NT with texts meant to be read out loud this dramatically changes things.

"But not everyone agrees. Some claim that Mark's Gospel is the first Christian book, based on the reference in Mark 13:14 where we find the parenthetical remark, 'let the reader understand.' Some assume that the 'reader' in question is the audience. But let us examine this assumption for a moment.

Both in Mark 13:14 and Revelation 1:3 the operative Greek words are *ho anaginōskōn*, a clear reference to a *single* reader, who in the Revelation text is clearly *distinguished* from the audience who are dubbed the hearers (plural!) of John's rhetoric. As Mark Wilson recently suggested in a public lecture at Ephesus, this surely is likely to mean that the singular reader is in fact a lector of sorts, someone who will be reading John's apocalypse out loud to various hearers.[1] We know that John is addressing various churches in Asia Minor, so it is quite impossible to argue that the reference to 'the

1. In a lecture delivered by him at a conference at Ephesus in May 2008 where Mark and Ben both spoke on the oral character of these NT texts.

reader' singular in Revelation 1:3 refers to the audience. It must refer to the person who will orally deliver this discourse to the audience of hearers.

"I suggest that we draw the same conclusion about the phrase in Mark 13:14, which in turn means that not even Mark's Gospel should be viewed as a text meant for private reading, much less the first real modern book. Rather Mark is reminding the lector, who will be orally delivering the Gospel, to help the audience understand the nature of what was happening when the temple in Jerusalem was destroyed. Oral texts often include such reminders for the ones delivering the discourse in question.

"As it turns out, it is never adequate to read the Bible in a modern translation with modern assumptions about written texts. Not only does the meaning of the text get lost in the translation, but the very spirit of the text gets lost when we don't recognize it as oral tradition. How do these insights help us as we begin the process of studying closely the Q document? Here are a few clues.

"First, we need to listen to the document! We need Aramaic experts to read the document to us in small doses so we can process and grasp how it was meant to be heard.

"Secondly, since the document is written in *scriptio continua* we need help separating the words and phrases and sentences. Up to this point we have relied on scholars like Joachim Jeremias or Maurice Casey to help us retroject a Greek text backwards into what might have been the original Aramaic. Not any more! We can work forward from the Aramaic original, bearing in mind that the Q document is literally the predecessor of the equivalent Greek passages in the Gospels so that here is where our discussion of the original words of Jesus should begin.

"Thirdly, once we have separated out the words, then we can study the purpose and meaning of the Q document. Is there an order to the sayings? Is there a plan to their arrangement?

"It is a new day, my friends! We have an exciting new document to study! Let's explore it in a new way! Thank you!" Grayson was grinning from ear to ear!

The pep talk was effective and the applause was generous. Grace came across the stage and gave Grayson a hug. Kahlil and Hannah joined them.

Kahlil boomed, "We had no idea you had become such a scholar!"

Grayson blushed. "God works in mysterious ways!"

58

EARLY WARNING SIGNS

KAHLIL EL SAID WAS by no means as spry as he used to be. For one thing, he had been shot only a few years prior.[1] For another, he had gone through a lot of emotional trauma after Hannah's assault.[2] Life was not easy for Kahlil who grew up on the streets of Jerusalem. But he had made quite a good name for himself as an antiquities dealer. With the sale of a first century menorah, Kahlil had become a multi-millionaire, which allowed him to endow Art West's research chest with a considerable amount of money. Although he loved his shop and modest home, he knew he would eventually have to sell the shop. And Hannah was eager to move to another home to raise her son Samuel.

As Hannah and Kahlil were driving back home from Grayson's lecture, Kahlil felt a sharp pain in his chest, causing him to take a deep breath. Hannah noticed the sudden heavy breathing.

"Is there something wrong, Father?"

In a moment he replied, "Oh it's probably nothing, just a little indigestion and heartburn, I imagine. I shouldn't have eaten that spicy hummus and bread for breakfast this morning. Anyway, it has passed now; let's talk about something else. What did you think of Grayson's lecture?"

"I found it fascinating. I suppose I have been so used to living in a world of texts that I had never considered the possibility of ancient texts

---

1. This story was told in the very first Art West adventure, *The Lazarus Effect*.
2. A tale told in the fifth Art West adventure, *Corinthian Leather*.

being unlike modern ones. The idea of 'oral texts' makes so much sense in a world full of people who could all listen but mostly could not read. One of the questions the lecture prompted in my mind is, how close is that Aramaic text to either one of the Gospels that contain that material?"

"Razor sharp question, my bright daughter! I remember Grace saying it was closer to the Matthean text of the Sermon on the Mount and other sayings of Jesus, but that's all I know."

"What impressed me most was the transformation in Grayson's life. Remember when he was just a hippie for Jesus here in Jerusalem years back. He has become a real scholar now, and I gather a respected archaeologist for some of the things he has discovered up at Caesarea Philippi."

"You're right, and I have to say, I didn't see this coming when I first met Grayson during the whole Lazarus tomb escapade."

The conversation continued all the way back to the old city. Kahlil, making a good show of things, jumped out of the car, went around the back, and opened the door for his daughter like a gentleman would do. He strode confidently with her through the Damascus Gate and down the alleys to their antiquities shop. Hannah made a mental note to make sure her father saw a doctor before long, because that chest pain episode might be more significant than just another bout of heartburn. She would have to wait and see on that one. For now, they were both glad to be home.

Once in the shop, it didn't take five minutes for the phone to ring. It was Art.

"Good afternoon, Kahlil. This is Art reporting on the trauma here in Izmir. I wish I could be calling under better circumstances."

"Old friend, you don't have to apologize about life's traumas. We have had our share—and while they don't make us healthier, they do make us wiser, I think."

"I certainly like your version better than Nietzsche's 'What does not kill me, makes me stronger,'" laughed Art. "The bottom line—she is improving by the hour. She is awake! I can sit by her bed and we can talk for a while before she falls asleep again. But those times are getting longer and longer."

"It's only been a couple of days, Art. Do not rush things. It is wiser to let healing proceed at its own pace—which is usually very, very slowly. Trust me." Kahlil remained silent for a moment and then added, "You know I sensed something was wrong. I just prayed all day Saturday for someone's healing, but it was evening before God lifted the burden on my heart."

"Saturday evening is when Mark Wilson came to the hospital and anointed Marissa with holy oil and laid hands upon her. It reminds me of the famous story in John 4 of Jesus and the centurion whose son or servant Jesus healed at a distance. When the soldier asked his companions whom he met on the road when the child began to get better, they told him the hour, and the centurion said it was precisely the hour when Jesus proclaimed, 'Your son will live.'"

"Well God is still doing the same miracles you know," said Kahlil. "He hasn't run out of power, so why should we be surprised."

Art laughed and said, "No reason! No reason at all! Thank you so much for praying. God used your prayers and Mark's to save my sweetheart. I owe you a lot."

"Actually, you owe God a lot; we are just helpers of the helpless. That's all. Shall I tell you some good local gossip?" offered Kahlil to break the tension.

"That would be a refreshing change of tune," laughed Art.

"Grayson Johnson, your protégé, gave the inaugural address at this new symposium Grace has begun here at Hebrew University on the Q document, and it was excellent! I was so impressed. I didn't realize he had become a full-fledged scholar, and not just one more digger in the dirt in the Holy Land."

"Grace has been keeping me informed of his progress, but this must have been his first major lecture. I'll bet he was as nervous as a cat on a hot tin roof."

"Yes, a little shaky at the start of the lecture, but he gained confidence as he went on. You have done well to encourage him, and you need to come and help Grace with this ongoing work if you can."

"I know in my heart now that we will come together. In the meantime, send my love to Hannah and Samuel."

"Until then, my friend. Next year in Jerusalem *ensh'allah*."

"As God's wills," repeated Art.

59

FAMILY TIME

PROGRESS WAS PAINFULLY SLOW. For the past several days, Art bounced back and forth between the hospital and the apartment lent him by Levent. Mel entertained everyone in the waiting room with enchanting tales of exotic destinations and hilarious stories about quirky tourists. She was now off on another tour. Mark stopped in periodically for impromptu prayer. And Marissa's parents found friends to stay with and promised not to leave until their daughter was up and about.

What better time to get to know the in-laws. He finally decided they were more afraid of him than he was of them. So the best thing to do was ask questions and convince them that he really was interested in knowing all the trivia about Marissa and her life. Once that was accomplished, they regaled Art with stories about Marissa and her older sister, Zehra, a doctor in their home town of Ankara.

According to Zeliha, her daughter Zehra was shy and, outside of her work, did not really have a social life. She lived for what she loved—medicine—doctoring her dolls and pets from an early age. Marissa had been the social animal from the first, with many friends and social activities, which gave Zeliha her gray hairs at an early age, or so she claimed. According to Zafer, with all those friends Marissa should have found a husband for Zehra! Both of them began telling fun stories about vacations in Antalya and balloon rides over Cappadocia. They often took the girls to archaeological sites. Marissa would scamper around in the ruins. Zehra would search out new plants and animals.

Monday found Art and Zafer having lunch together in a nearby café; hospital food was getting old. "Marissa has worked very hard to get where she is in life professionally. She is a Type A personality! Maybe it is a good thing that you both are in the same line of work. There is much you can share—but will it be shared equally? How does my Marissa fit into your life plans?" Zafer asked quite plainly.

Art smiled. "You're right—we are both Type A personalities! We've learned to be very, very independent people, and now we're learning how to depend on one another. It's a major adjustment at our age. We are both used to having our own way, doing our own thing and being in charge."

"We come from a family where the wife is allowed to have her own career—this is rather unique in some parts of the Middle East. We have worked hard here in Turkey to develop a society that treats women as they should be treated—as equals—not as subservient slaves. Marissa values her freedom to have her own life," reminded Zafer.

"Yes, Turkey is unique—and I can tell you that it's my favorite country to visit—and now I can call it my home away from home," responded Art earnestly.

"Your life will change a great deal—you will have to determine what the new normal is going to look like. The two of you cannot just go back to business as usual. Have you even settled on a home base? I can tell you that my Zeliha wishes it were Ankara," laughed Zafer.

"We talked about spending the academic year in the States, and our summers in Turkey and other places in the Middle East. Of course, Marissa can't sit around while I'm teaching. I'm hoping and praying that she can find a research or teaching post—there are lots of big name universities in the Durham-Raleigh area. For now we also want to rent a flat in Istanbul."

"I would not ask about children, but Zeliha made me do it!"

"I understand. My mother certainly won't stop asking about that for a long while," sighed Art. "One thing I can say—Marissa will have the main say on that issue!"

"And that's how it should be," agreed Zafer. "It is sad to see a Muslim woman living at the mercy of her husband and especially the mother-in-law who dictates when and how many children the family will have. When women are empowered to take charge of their family—everyone is the winner," said Zafer forcefully. "We will be surprised if Marissa doesn't want children, but who knows these days? She is a modern woman, and we are proud of that. We will not interfere!"

"Thank you—Marissa doesn't need the pressure right now. Her healing, physically and mentally, may take longer than any of us realize," said Art a bit worried.

The two sat in silence mulling over the events that brought them to this luncheon table in the middle of Izmir.

"Let me pay the bill," said Zafer reaching for his wallet. "Ah, but this reminds me to say that if we can help financially, please tell us. I understand that you actually arranged a million dollar ransom for our daughter. We can't put a value on Marissa's life but your willingness to pay such a ransom is, well . . . I don't have the words," said Zafer nearly in tears.

"Now I can put the check safely back into the account. The fund for my archaeology study is substantial—and I expect that we'll use that money to dig at locations near and dear to Marissa's heart as well. I appreciate your offer of help, but I can assure you that we are in a good place financially."

The conversation went on for an hour and more, and Art silently was thanking God for having in-laws he could actually talk to, especially considering their cultural and religious differences. Despite the recent trauma, God had put Art into a blessed situation in so many ways, and he was deeply grateful and hopeful about the future. The most recent events had forced Art to the very end of his own personal and emotional resources, and at the same time forced him to realize how helpless he was to control or cope with forces larger than he could deal with alone or even with the help of friends. In short, he knew more than ever how much he needed to rely on the Lord, and not just in times of crisis.

60

THE PATRIARCH'S PLEA

PATRIARCH BARTHOLOMEW, BEING THE pastoral type that he was, decided to call Art West for a report. Art was sitting by Marissa's bedside when his phone vibrated. He answered the phone as he strode down the hall back to the waiting area.

"Professor West, this is the Patriarch. I hope it is appropriate for me to call and inquire about your wife."

"Yes, your Eminence! So much has happened since Marissa was kidnapped on Saturday. We have spent the last several days here in the hospital in Izmir. Fortunately, she is now truly on the mend. I'm hoping she will be discharged by the end of the week. We may go back to Istanbul or to Ankara to be near her parents."

"Clearly the healing of your wife is of first importance. Do you feel up to talking about the matter of the House of Mary? If not, I will understand," said the Patriarch gently.

"I would be happy to talk about this amazing situation! My first thought is, let me get together several Mary experts, just a few who are trustworthy. I will let you come up with the name of the Orthodox scholar but I have one Catholic, Matthew Levering, and one Protestant, Scot McKnight, in mind, both of whom care deeply about the historical Mary. As you may know, I did my doctoral work on women in the NT, and so I also care about this matter a great deal, and do not wish any shame to come on your church from a callous public airing of the matter. I suggest we set up a symposium at the end of the summer. I will come and chair the program, but it will be private and the results confidential. Who knows? Perhaps we will conclude it's not really Mary the mother of Jesus you found. After all, there were other women named Mary in Jesus' band of followers. And there were other women named Mary at the cross as well according to John 19. Right?"

"To be honest," said Bartholomew, "that thought had not crossed my mind. The corpse could certainly be another Mary, or even a friend or companion of Mary!"

"The point is, there is no need for a rush to judgment. Are the bones somewhere removed from the public eye and in safe keeping?"

"You may laugh at this, but we have put them in the charnel house at the Monastery at Sumela. There are other bones stored in that vaulted burial chamber. They will be safe there."

This response puzzled Art. "But Sumela, which I visited last summer, is a public museum, not a proper monastery!"

"Yes and no. In fact you will not believe what happened just a few Sundays ago. The government of Turkey allowed Christians to pray for three hours on a Sunday at the Sumela Greek Orthodox monastery for the first time since the country's creation. The government finally recognizes that this gesture toward Christians might improve Turkey's record on religious tolerance and even boost tourism. During the service we had such a strong sense of God's blessed presence with us.

"The Turkish papers quoted me as saying, 'After 88 years, the tears of the Virgin Mary have stopped flowing.' What the report does not say, is that we were allowed to rebury an 'anonymous' saint on that same occasion. All the

government knew was that it was an ancient Christian, and so we put Mary out of harm's way, where no tourist would look, in the charnel house burial vault in the very back of the monastery which no one visits. She is the only one there, and she is under lock and key. I am the only one with the key!"

"I'm impressed. I so wish I could have been there," said Art a bit wistfully.

"I am sending you right now a few shots from the monastery. Pay particular attention to the last one. I take it as an image of the Spirit re-entering the monastery after so many years. You have to admit, it is a good place to put her.

"The last shot is of the pathway pilgrims take up to the monastery, and it was taken just after we transported Mary's holy remains to the monastery and were heading back down the path to the car park."

"I can only say, Holy Smokes!" enthused Art having seen the pictures. "At least Mary's remains have now ascended to a high place in Turkey, if it is *that* Mary's remains. Certainly, no one will be looking for her there."

"No. But I should not keep you. Once things are better for you, please give me a call, and we will set up the conclave you suggested right here in Istanbul. Then we can give Mary our full attention."

"Yes your Eminence. She deserves no less."

"I'm glad you think so. God bless you and keep you. Until then."

"And you." As he hung up the phone Art thought, now there is a Christian leader admirable and honest in every way. I will look forward to working with him and I'm sure Marissa will as well.

61

BABY TALK

BY THE END OF the week, Marissa was ready to leave the hospital. Her ankle was mending well and Marissa had mastered the art of using a cane for a while. Her remaining kidney was functioning just fine. Her headaches were gone, and there was no sign of any brain damage, nor was there any sign of internal bleeding. In fact, there was no indication of any spleen damage. Art bragged that she was a "medical miracle." He had no problem reminding the doctors and nurses of the events of last Saturday night. The daily parade of visitors was impressive, as friends and relatives came in and out, and the huge bank of flowers from home and abroad that surrounded Marissa's bed was testimony to how much she was loved by many.

Just that morning she got a call from Hannah in Jerusalem renewing the invitation for them to come and stay in Jerusalem. And they both knew that Art was eager to see the Q manuscript—although a trip to Paris was still essential to see the original. Grace called to "scold" them both for not being at the symposium. And, of course, the guest room was always ready at the Cohen compound.

They thought about playing it safe and going back to Ankara. Or they could try to manage on their own at Marissa's studio apartment in Istanbul and start looking for a larger place. Or . . .

"Arthur, you Americans have an old cowboy saying—something like, if you fall off your horse, get back on!"

"Right, but I'm at a loss to imagine where you are going with this."

"I'm going back to Kushadasi! In my mind, we never properly finished our honeymoon. If I remember I was running on the beach, and you were on the phone, and we were hurrying back to Istanbul, and then. . . . Well, let's not even talk about that. I don't want our honeymoon to end on that note! Let's go back and do it right!"

"Are you really saying that you want to go back to the Sea Pines, breathe in the sea air, walk on the beach, enjoy the food . . . ."

"Exactly! Do you think I'm crazy!"

"I think you're brilliant!"

~

Three days later, they were indeed sitting on the beach late in the evening watching the sun go down across the Aegean Sea.

"I think the Lord has given me a new outlook on life," began Marissa. "I was making plans in my head in a spirit of fear—what if this happened or what if that happened."

"And now you are planning to go boldly where you've never gone before?" asked Art. "I hope I can go with you!"

"Well, there's no way I can put my plans into action without you! I want a child, Arthur. I want our child," she said softly.

Art smiled, wrinkled up his nose and said, "Fine by me! I'll be a bit old by the time he—or she—goes to college. If you're okay with our child having a silver-haired Dad, then let's see what we can produce!"

"I predict we are going to produce our own little miracle!" promised Marissa.

~

THE END

AUTHOR'S NOTE

THE ARCHAEOLOGICAL INFORMATION IN this novel is accurate to the best of our knowledge. I recently visited Nemrut and Göbeckli Tepe in Eastern Turkey. Both Ann and I have been to Ephesus, Istanbul, Kushadasi, and Izmir a number of times. The excavations of the terrace houses in Ephesus are truly remarkable. The Chora Church in Istanbul is one of the great marvels of early Christian art and architecture, and most of the time when you see famous pictures of Christ in glory in advertisements for Christian touring in Turkey, the images do not come from Hagia Sophia, but rather from the lesser known Chora Church. The Sea Pines Hotel in Kushadasi is an excellent choice for tourists. The Ataturk monument does overlook Izmir.

The death of Mary is not recorded in the scripture. Catholic and Orthodox tradition and doctrine support the Assumption—that Mary was taken bodily into heaven possibly before but more probably after her death. In the Roman Catholic tradition, Pope Pius XII left open the question of whether Mary died before she was taken into heaven. The early Church Fathers suggest that she died first, and most believe that she did. The Orthodox focus on the Dormition of the Blessed Virgin Mary (the Theotokos) which emphasizes her death. At that point, her soul was taken into heaven but her body was only assumed into heaven three days later. Regardless, we should have an empty tomb! The Assumption of Mary is shared in both Eastern and Western Catholic Churches, the Eastern Orthodox Churches, Coptic Churches, parts of the Anglican Communion and Continuing Anglican Churches.

The House of Mary is a pilgrimage site in Ephesus. Since opposing traditions believe Mary was in Jerusalem at the end of her days on earth, there is a competing site for the Assumption—the Church of the Sepulcher of Mary at the foot of the Mount of Olives in Jerusalem. Since I have made a case that the Beloved Disciple was Lazarus, not John, I am not taking a stand as to where Mary was buried!

Obviously part of the fiction of the novel is the discovery of a body at the House of Mary. Such a discovery would indeed cause a major dilemma for Catholicism and the Orthodox tradition as well. Note that we left open the identification of the body—more than one Mary played a role in Jesus' life. Nevertheless, such a discovery is not impossible and the Sumela Monastery which is dedicated to the Virgin Mary would make for an interesting final resting place!

As for the so-called Q document, it has certainly not been found, but this is also possible since we do know there were collections of Jesus' sayings made in the first and second centuries A.D. The Q hypothesis has more going for it than the arguments for the dependence of Luke on Matthew or vice versa. Though it is later, the Gospel of Thomas gives us a concrete example of the sort of document that Q must have been. Grayson's lecture at the end of the novel is based on my research on Q which can be found in *Jesus the Sage* (2000) and *What's in a Word* (2009).

Readers have noticed that sometimes real persons are mentioned in these novels. The President of Turkey since 2007 is indeed Abdullah Gül, although the political power is in the hands of the Prime Minister, Recep Tayyip Erdoğan. Patriarch Bartholomew I has been the Archbishop of Constantinople since 1991. Along with many believers, we support his efforts to reopen the Halki Seminary. I have fond memories of meeting this very special man. We hope that our portrayals of various real figures are accurate and respectful.

Our friends surface in the novels frequently and, so far as we know, they enjoy being part of the stories even when we do embellish their personalities! Dr. Mark Wilson is the director of the Asia Minor Research Center in Antalya, Turkey. Reverend James Howell is the senior pastor of Myers Park United Methodist Church in Charlotte, North Carolina. The banker, Richard Character, is based on our friend Richard Carriker, himself a retired banker. William Arnold is really Dr. Bill Arnold, Old Testament Professor at Asbury Theological Seminary. Grace Levine Cohen is loosely based on Dr. Amy-Jill Levine, a distinguished New Testament scholar at Vanderbilt University Divinity School. Levent Oral is the owner of Tutku Tours where Meltem Çitci (or Ciftci) is indeed one of his best tour guides—we can attest to that on numerous of our trips!

The character of Joyce West is strongly based on my mother, Joyce West Witherington. My sister, Laura Joyce Witherington, lives and works in Jacksonville, Florida. Our children, Christy and David, were reworked as twin cousins. Our beloved Christy died in 2012 at the age of 32. David, now 31 at this writing, is living with his wife Emily in North Wales, PA and working as a computer specialist. This book is dedicated to David and Emily on the occasion of their wedding October 20, 2012.

Ben Witherington, August 2013